Summer of Irreverence:
The Rock Star

by

Cathrine Goldstein

The New York Artists Series

Summer of Irreverence: The Rock Star

Cover Art by *Angela Anderson*

The Wild Rose Press, Inc.
PO Box 708
Adams Basin, NY 14410-0708
Visit us at www.thewildrosepress.com

Publishing History
First Champagne Rose Edition, 2016
Print ISBN 978-1-5092-0867-8
Digital ISBN 978-1-5092-0868-5

The New York Artists Series
Published in the United States of America

"How did you go through life
with that name…?" Malcolm's eyes flashed with happiness. "I mean, if I wrote it people would crucify me. What were your parents thinking?"

Summer froze.

"I mean, do they love you at all?" Malcolm chuckled.

Summer's feet refused to move, and her arms lay limp at her side.

"Summer?" Malcolm's smile faded. "Sum?"

The sound of her nickname spoken by Malcolm did her in. She desperately fought the mounting tears.

Malcolm stared at her. "It's not your name you're upset about, is it?"

Summer clenched her jaw and shook her head.

"I'm sorry." His voice was low and modulated.

She nodded, looking at Malcolm, and wanting, for the first time ever, to have someone make it all okay. To have him make it all okay.

Malcolm grew quiet. They stood there for whole minutes. "I'm sorry if I touched on a sore subject. Really."

Summer stared at him—this man who had everything except the answer she needed. How could he be so closed off? How could he care so little about the pain of another living creature?

He stepped forward then, as if reading her mind, took her hand gently, and leaned over, speaking quietly into her ear. "It's not that I don't care." Those few words found a place deep in Summer's soul.

Malcolm stood tall, and Summer's eyes followed him. He reached out and stroked her cheek. "But I've got nothing more to give than today."

Praise for Cathrine Goldstein

"*The Hunger Games* meets *Divergent*! This pair of books was so engaging…I couldn't put them down…"

~*Kovescene of the Mind*

~*~

"I highly recommend this book—it's freaking amazing."

~*Perks of Being a Book Girl*

~*~

"I'm completely blown away by how original this story truly is…I beg you give these a go…"

~*Mama Reads Hazel Sleeps*

~*~

"The Letting series is amazing…all elements that you look for when you read. Adventure, love, mystery, action… really everything."

~*The Cubicle Escapee*

~*~

"Woo. What a ride. I almost think The Letting is going to be the next big hit series"

~*Book Lover's Report*

~*~

"…A gripping new novel that will enchant readers from the very first page…very well written book with a fascinating and original plot."

~*A Dream Within A Dream*

Dedications

As always, for Jay, Penelope, and Pickle (Sarah).
Thank you.
~*~
And a huge "thank you" to my wonderful editor,
Fran Sevilla!!!!!

Chapter One

"That's it. I want to lose my virginity…" Summer threw herself against the breakfast bar where Jeanette was picking at a meal of cottage cheese and strawberries.

Jeanette nearly choked as she laid down her fork and stared at her friend. "Excuse me?"

"You heard me." Summer twirled a long blonde lock absentmindedly, as her mind wandered to thoughts of…someone else… She sighed deeply; her tiny body felt unusually heavy and lethargic, like she needed another eight hours of sleep, but at the same time, her thoughts were running wild. She had been in the city for a few days now, and it was high time to get on with her plan.

"Okay," Jeanette drew in a deep breath and gave her full attention to Summer. "Um, Summer, I'm not sure how to tell you this, but just 'cause a relationship ends, it doesn't mean you're back to being a virgin. Virginity is not self-renewing like…like a frog's legs." She giggled.

Summer rolled her eyes. "You're in a good mood this morning." She plopped down on a stool across from Jeanette. "And that's a myth by the way."

"What is?"

"That frogs can regenerate, or uh, regrow a limb."

"Really?" Jeanette eyed her friend skeptically.

"Yup." Summer picked up an orange from the fruit bowl and tossed it from hand to hand. She closed her eyes and mentally dissected her plan once more. Was it feasible? Or was she absolutely crazy?

"But what about Rocko?"

Summer opened her eyes and shook her head. "Rocko your frog? From when we were kids?"

Jeanette nodded. She took a bite of her fat-free, lactose-free cottage cheese, and grimaced.

Summer reached across the bar and took Jeanette's hand, hesitating for a moment. Although they were grown-ups now, she still felt remarkably like a nasty troll telling a six year old there is no Santa Claus.

"Um, Jeanette…" Summer approached this carefully. "It's time you knew. Rocko…he didn't actually live as long as you thought. After the…accident…your dad replaced him. And then again, many times after that."

"Many times?"

Jeanette's face fell. Darn it. The last thing Summer wanted was to make her friend unhappy—even if it all happened ages ago, and even though the situation was just a teensy bit comical. Summer squeezed Jeanette's hand.

"I'm sorry, Jean. Your dad didn't want you to know. He didn't want you to be upset."

"But I was sure Rocko was the one. You know how many times I kissed that damned frog…correction, *those* damned frogs, trying to get my prince?"

Summer giggled, raising her eyebrows. "Well, you've got him now."

"That's true. Elijah is pretty awesome."

"Yes, I would say he was worth all the kisses you

laid on those poor frogs." Summer tucked her hair behind her ear and chewed her lip. She took a deep breath. This was as good a time as any. "And uh, Jean, speaking of Elijah—"

Jeanette shook her head. "Wait a sec. We can talk about him later. You can't make an announcement like that and leave me hanging. What's this, 'I want to lose my virginity' crap all about?"

Summer's cheeks warmed as panic began rising in her. She swallowed it back. Think, think, think. "Green Anole Lizards."

"Excuse me? Your sudden proclamation about losing your virginity, which I know happened in high school by the way, has to do with a lizard?"

Summer shook her head. "Ew. No. No. The Green Anole Lizard can regenerate its tail. It's not the same as the original tail that consisted of bones, this new tail is primarily cartilage and—"

"Summer." Jeanette put up her hand. "I want to talk about your love life, not…lizards. If this is your idea of conversation, I'm beginning to get a glimpse into your life with the great Dr. Brad Parker."

"Ugh…don't remind me." Summer looked off, out the window.

Outside, the first rays of dawn came peeking through the blinds, brightening the drab yellow apartment, and lifting Summer's spirits. It was amazing, the power the sun could have. Even here, trapped in a concrete world she really didn't know, the sun offered Summer some welcomed normalcy.

Summer pulled herself up from the breakfast bar and walked to the widow. She pushed up the window leading to the fire escape, and immediately, the hot, sticky Manhattan morning found its way in, like a hungry alley cat. Darn, it was warm. It seemed even the nicest of apartments weren't immune to a hot Manhattan morning. Summer pulled off her robe, tossing it onto the couch. Even from across the room she could feel Jeanette's disapproving gaze.

"Even in summer, huh?" Jeanette tossed her head toward Summer's pajamas.

Summer chewed her lip.

"All right. Come on, Sum."

Jeanette patted the stool next to her, and Summer made her way over.

"Is this about the great, Doctor Brad?"

Summer shook her head vehemently. Then she paused. "Not directly."

"Then tell me. Because last I checked, you were the one who ended your long-term relationship with Brad, the hot vet-slash-professor who wanted to marry you. Yes?"

"Yes."

"Are you having second thoughts?"

"No." Although Summer couldn't put a finger on her melancholy, of this, she was certain. She did not miss Brad—in the least.

"Well, then what?" Jeanette twirled a strawberry from its stem. It popped free of her hand and rolled along the counter, leaving red streaks down the white quartz.

Summer snatched the strawberry and grabbed a dishtowel to wipe away the red stain. "We've got to grab that stain before it sets."

Jeanette shrugged. "Leave it. Elijah will buy me a new counter. Actually, he'll buy me a new kitchen."

Jeanette smiled coyly.

Summer folded the dishtowel and cocked her head. "You really like him, huh?"

"It's that obvious?"

"Jean, this is me. I've known you since second grade. I've been with you through every relationship you've had. Every teacher you've dated...every dad I talked you away from when we babysat..."

"Yeah, you were always the sensible one. Who would have thought you'd end up dating your professor."

Summer buried her head in her hands. "Ugh, don't remind me. And you would have dated professors too if you went to college."

"Oh no, you don't." Jeanette clapped her hands together as if she was silencing a barking dog. "No way. I'm not getting into this now. I am very happy with my chosen career."

"I know, it's just you have a mind for business and—"

Jeanette held up her hand. "Tell you what. You spare me the model talk, and I'll spare you the pajama talk. Deal?"

"Deal." Summer smiled.

"So, why this sudden proclamation? And what the hell does it mean?" Jeanette held out her bowl of strawberries, but Summer shook her head.

"No, thanks. That's your food for the day, I wouldn't dare."

Jeanette rolled her eyes. "Sum, fess up. What's the deal?"

"I just..." Summer chose her words carefully. "I just, I've never had my world...*rocked*...you know?"

Jeanette stared. "Brad wasn't good?"

Summer's cheeks began to heat. "It's not that he wasn't good. It's that he just kind of…was."

"He sure is handsome, I'll give you that."

"Yeah…" Summer looked off.

"And tall."

"Yeah."

"And an older man. What is he, like thirty-five?"

"Thirty-six."

"Well, what?" Jeanette abandoned her breakfast and looked closely at Summer. "You can't lead me this far and then leave me. What a tease, Sum."

Summer shot Jeanette an incredulous look and sighed. She settled in, resting her hands on the counter. She hated the idea of discussing details of her personal life, even with her best friend. But she needed help from Jeanette, and to get the kind of help she needed, she would have to let Jeanette in. Her knee began to bounce nervously. "All right."

Jeanette gulped her black coffee. "Really? Really?" Jeanette wiped her hands in that same dishtowel. "You never spill. Ever. Okay, let me have it."

"Brad was…sort of…weak."

"In bed?" Jeanette spun Summer's stool around to face her.

"No…" Summer shook her head. "Well, yes, I suppose. Well, everywhere, I guess. I mean, he was always so hung up on being my professor and proving to me I was smart, but in the most patronizing way. He would yell in surgery, but after…he was just…blah. And through it all, he kind of forgot to be a man."

"No…" Jeanette's eyes grew wider with every word Summer spoke.

"What I mean is he was always respectful. But sometimes he was a bit too respectful. You know?"

Jeanette nodded along, nearly salivating.

"He was so concerned I was his equal, everywhere but in the operating room, he forgot that women sometimes want to be…you know…" Summer tipped her head hoping Jeanette would fill in the rest—silently.

"Had?"

Summer nodded, her cheeks on fire. "Yes. I…I know I'm smart. And I know eventually I'll make a fairly good living as a veterinary surgeon…as soon as I pay off these student loans. But I'd still like it if he showed a little…manliness around me. Pick up the check at dinner instead of splitting it; insist on driving the darn car once in awhile; stop asking my permission on every move…quit asking me how I'm feeling about everything…" Summer's chest heaved as the words fell from her mouth. "And for heaven's sake, initiate once in awhile, you know?"

Jeanette crammed cottage cheese into her mouth, riveted.

Summer jumped to her feet and stomped away. "And when we do, do it…then make a little effort. Not always the same position, for the same amount of time." She whipped around to face Jeanette. "Do you know in the year and a half we were together we never…did it…anywhere but his bed? Never. And I'm not talking about outside the bedroom, I mean never on the floor, never against a wall, never from behind…"

"Always missionary?" Jeanette asked timidly.

"I wish." Summer ran her hand through her hair. "Then he would be a man."

"Then how?"

"How else would the great, caring Doctor Brad do it? Side by side. Always. So we're equals. That's got to be the most unfulfilling position ever for a woman." Summer threw up her hands in exasperation.

"It doesn't have to be."

"No?" Summer's eyes landed on Jeanette.

"No."

"Oh goodness." Summer collapsed back into her seat. "Guess I've had that bottled up for a bit. Sorry."

"It's…okay." Jeanette stared, flabbergasted.

Summer dropped her chin, and spoke to the floor. "He's the exact opposite of what I need. I need someone who respects my work, but still treats me like I'm a woman. You know?"

"If you don't think he respects your work, then why the job offer?"

"It's a game." Summer sighed. "He's on a power trip. And he's the best around, so if I want to make a name for myself, quickly, I'm going to have to take it."

Jeanette nodded. "Will you be able to work together amicably?"

Summer shrugged. "We'll have to. I just finished my residency with him, and we were okay. Unless…" She stared off.

"Unless, what? Sum?"

"He's kind of a bully in the operating room. He makes me second guess my decisions. Even when I'm completely right. I think he really overcompensates for being such a wimp in real life."

"I've just got to say…I'm a little surprised. I thought Brad was the greatest guy ever, he seems so…"

"I know," Summer nodded, throwing her hands into the air. "Looks can be deceiving, I guess."

"But just a few days ago you were singing his praises—when you were at the clinic…"

"That's true." Summer looked up. "He is an excellent surgeon. But I'm afraid that's just not enough to build a life on, you know?"

"Yeah." Jeanette nodded.

"I respect his work, but that's it—not his work ethic and not him."

"You don't think you could ever love him?" Jeanette asked these words carefully, through her lashes. She avoided direct eye contact.

"Jeanette." Summer focused on Jeanette's eyes. Her shoulders slumped, and her voice modulated to its normal tone. She smiled sweetly. Jeanette was a good friend. The best. But she just never seemed to understand the truth about love. "You know I don't believe in love. I'm sorry, but love just doesn't exist. Scientifically, it makes no sense. You know what the purpose of the human heart is? To *beat*. That's why people who believe in it, find love hurts so much—because they center their feelings on our most violent organ. Look, I'm sorry to be such a downer to you and all the romantics out there, but I'm a doctor. A scientist. Truth be told, I know what the heart does, and it has nothing to do with a serotonin release that makes one feel temporarily euphoric."

"Wow." Jeanette shook her head. "I'm glad you never considered a career as a romance writer."

Summer rolled her eyes.

"So…" Jeanette was obviously trying to get back on track. "Can I ask why now? Why you're deciding you need to be…had…right now? And what's your plan? I know you, Sum. You've always got a plan."

Summer sighed. How could she make a woman like Jeanette—with her long black hair, icy blue eyes, and full red lips—understand this longing she was feeling? Jeanette was gorgeous, a high fashion model with a portfolio brimming with magazine covers. She oozed confidence and wore haute couture as effortlessly as most women wear yoga clothes. And, above all, Jeanette was a magnet for men.

Summer, on the other hand, was nothing like Jeanette. Summer had long, wavy blonde hair and eyes the color of jade. She was thin but curvy, with full breasts and round hips, not at all graceful and angular like Jeanette. At five six, Summer wasn't short, but those measly four inches elevated Jeanette into a different stratosphere, and therefore, a different life.

And part of that different life included Jeanette's newest and most powerful accessory, Elijah, her boyfriend, who also just happened to be the business manager for the world's hottest band. The band Summer needed access to…

"Sum? Want to tell me what's gotten into you?" Jeanette stared at Summer and then looked at the face of her watch.

"We can talk later." Darn. She was losing her chance. "You don't need to waste your time on my moods."

"Oh, no," Jeanette shook her head. "I've got time. Spill it. You've always been so…serious. Why exactly are you feeling this way?"

Summer shrugged.

"What's going on, Sum? The anniversary?"

"Maybe…" Here it was, Memorial Day weekend— the unofficial start of the summer season, and the official end of Summer's life as she had known it. "It's the twelfth anniversary of my parents' deaths. I don't know. That number just feels so big." Summer whispered through an achy throat. She knew she didn't need to say it. Jeanette had been with her through every horrific moment. But still. Summer looked up. "The twelfth anniversary; I'm twenty-eight, and I'm a vet. The one thing I said I would be—"

"Since second grade."

"Yeah." Summer nodded. "And I seem to have everything. I even had a guy who looked great on paper. But inside…"

"Summer," Jeanette reached out and took Summer's hand. "I think what you're telling me is, in all this time of setting up the perfect life, you forgot to live."

"Yes." Summer nodded.

"So why now?"

"I don't start my new job, and go back to Dr. Brad, until Labor Day. Labor Day weekend we have a veterinary convention here in the city. So I have from now, until Labor Day, to live."

Jeanette raised her coffee cup in a toast. "Well it sounds like a perfect summer to me."

Summer leveled her eyes on Jeanette. "Thank you, again."

"For what?"

"For letting me stay here. I know I cramp your style."

"Sum, I'm thrilled you're here. We can always go to Elijah's place when we need some privacy. And besides, watching you kick back and let go a bit is going to make this a summer for me to remember."

Jeanette grinned. "So, any ideas?"

"One." Summer ignored her racing heart. "And I need your help."

"Okay…" Jeanette tilted her head.

Before she could lose her nerve, Summer lurched forward and grabbed a newspaper off the breakfast bar. She turned to the society page. She pointed at a picture. "Him. I need you to get me to him."

"Donald Trump?" Jeanette narrowed her brows.

"What?" Summer turned the paper to study the picture. "No. *Him*. This picture."

Jeanette shook her head. "Malcolm Angel? The lead singer of the hottest band around?"

"Not just any band. Elijah's band. I know you see Malcolm all the time, Jean. Come on..."

"Summer, are you serious?"

"Out of my league?" Summer felt her dreams deflate as she stared wistfully at the paper.

"No, no…" Jeanette shook her head. "It's not that at all. It's just… this is the big time, you know?"

"You don't think I'm attractive enough." Summer sunk back into herself and drew her knees up onto her stool. She hugged herself.

"Summer," Jeanette dropped the tone of her voice. "I think you're way out of his league. This guy, Sum, he's bad news. A girl in every port and all that."

"But that's why he's so perfect. I can be…had…" Summer was still struggling with the word, "and then we can both move on, back to our own lives."

"As long as you understand you will probably be expected to move on about seven minutes after he's done."

Summer gritted her teeth. "Fine by me."

"Summer…"

Jeanette's voice was soft and kind, and Summer knew she was trying to talk her out of it.

"I don't want to see you get hurt here."

"I…won't." Summer spoke with as much conviction as she could. She swallowed, hard. "Jeanette. Look. I promise I'm not a dope. I know what sleeping with a man like this could potentially mean. That is, if he'd even want me. I mean, look at his date." Summer spun the picture to her friend.

"Christy. She's with my agency." Jeanette turned the paper back to Summer. "And for the record, she didn't sleep with him."

"Why not?" Summer's eyes widened.

"Because she was only there for the publicity. Summer…"

"Jeanette. I need this. Please. Just introduce me. He probably won't even look at me twice. If, by some miracle, he does take me up on my offer, then I'll use every possible protection to keep myself safe."

"It's not your body I'm worried about."

Summer tilted her head.

Jeanette sighed. "Why him?"

"Because he's incredibly sexy. And he is the polar opposite of Brad. And look at him." Summer placed her finger against his picture. She stared at his tan skin and his dark eyes filled with danger. Oh yes, he was absolutely bad news. "I don't care what lyrics he writes, that's a man who doesn't believe in love."

"Yes," Jeanette sighed. "I would think all of those things are true."

"And because I have never before encountered someone who seems so irreverent."

"Is that what this is?"

"Yes. My summer of irreverence. Goodness knows, I need it. All I ever do is play by the rules."

Jeanette nodded in agreement.

Summer bit the inside of her lip as she went on. "Malcolm Angel uses slang and curses in public."

Jeanette fought back her grin. "Summer, if that's your marker for irreverence, I can hook you up with the guy at the deli across the street. He speaks just like that, and he'll be a lot less hassle."

Summer cocked her head.

Jeanette shook hers, sighing. "Well, if you're serious, the first thing you'll have to do is stop using words like that."

"Like what?"

"Like, irreverence. He won't know what it means."

"Oh come on. The man writes his own music. He's the poet laureate of our generation. I think he knows the meanings of a few basic words."

Jeanette sat there, staring. "Don't do it, Sum."

"I have to, Jean." Summer's voice grew low and breathy.

"No, I mean, don't make this the moment you choose to believe in love."

Summer threw her head back, laughing. "Don't worry, Jean. There's absolutely no chance of that."

Chapter Two

Malcolm Angel loved early morning runs, and this morning, despite the oppressive heat that sat heavily on a wakening Manhattan, was no exception. Malcolm grinned to himself as he swerved gracefully—hood over his head, dark glasses hiding his eyes—through Central Park. He liked the heat, the extra punch it packed…he liked pushing himself to the limit…he liked, disappearing. He loved the anonymity of Manhattan, and he knew because of it, he could never and would never make anywhere else his home—despite the houses his management made him buy in various locations throughout the world.

"C'mon, boy," Malcolm patted his leg for Winston to catch up. The one thing Malcolm loved most about these runs was that he was able to share them with his best friend, Winston. Malcolm chuckled. Nope, he could never admit to anyone that here he was, the poet laureate of romance, and his greatest love had four paws and a wagging tail.

Most people knew Malcolm loved animals, but they didn't know about Winston. Malcolm made sure of it. He guarded his relationship with Winston like some celebrities shelter their children. Malcolm had no desire to risk Winston's life when some deranged lunatic tries to dognap him for ransom money. Malcolm shivered despite his perspiration. He shook his head. What a life.

Sure he had hoped for his celebrity and spent countless years honing his craft—but he also absolutely understood the expression: "Be careful what you wish for, you just might get it."

Pound, pound, pound. The corner of Malcolm's mouth turned up into a half grin. Thirty-nine years old, and damn, he was just reaching his peak. He looked down at Winston who was panting to keep up, his hips moving stiffly, like the Tin Man before Dorothy found the oil can. Malcolm looked away. Winston was absolutely fine—he was like Malcolm, incredibly strong—no matter what their ages.

Malcolm sidestepped a large rock in the path, realizing his grin took over his entire face. So maybe he was feeling a little bit cocky this morning. But it was okay. For a musician, he was humble. And Malcolm Angel wasn't just any musician. He was one of the most successful and famous rock stars on the planet. And he maintained that title year after year. As other musicians faded away, he held on strong, with new hit after new hit. It was a hell of a lot of work, but Malcolm had become more than a singer, he was a poet—the poet of romantic love. Malcolm chuckled to himself as he ran. It was so ironic. All of it. How could he be the poet of romantic love when he didn't know a damned thing about it?

Malcolm looked up at the sky. There was something in the air today—something freeing, which, considering the date, was incredibly odd. Malcolm shook his head. No. He whizzed through his run. If it wasn't that Winston was struggling, he would have taken the long route around the reservoir. Instead, he took a shortcut. Malcolm liked that he knew every nuance of the park, and he adored the feel of the untrustworthy clock that guided Manhattan—it reminded him of how he ran his own life. Maybe whatever it was that needed doing wasn't done on anyone else's schedule, but it would, eventually, get done.

Keeping a watchful eye on Winston, Malcolm pressed a bit harder. Okay, maybe neither of them was running as quickly as they used to, but it didn't matter. He didn't want to exhaust Winston. Eighteen was old for a Golden Lab, but Malcolm chose not to think about it. He pushed it from his mind as he did so many other thoughts. Some of the guys from the band asked Malcolm why he kept a Lab in a city like New York, but with the size of Malcolm's apartment, frankly, he could have kept a racehorse locked inside, no problem.

Surefooted, Malcolm dodged a rain puddle, but Winston charged right through. "Atta boy." Malcolm petted Winston's head as they ran, and Winston barked and yapped happily in response. "Not too bad for a couple of old guys, huh?"

Winston dashed ahead, and Malcolm spoke as they ran. "No one else understands, huh, boy? Forget all the work and stress of relationships, that's all you truly need in life—one good friend. Man's best friend, right?"

Winston barked his reply, and Malcolm shook his head.

"It's our secret, boy. Can't let anyone know I don't believe most of the crap I sing about."

Winston barked in agreement.

"Good boy," Malcolm finished his run with a sprint, and doubled back to get Winston. He rubbed

Winston's back. "I know my secret's safe with you. C'mon," Malcolm tossed his head in the opposite direction. "Let's hit the juice bar. I've got a long, dehydrating night ahead."

Winston yelped in agreement.

****

"Jeanette?" Summer fanned her friend with the paper. "Jean? You okay?"

Jeanette snapped to. "Yeah, fine. It's just…you're sure? As in, really sure?"

Summer took Jeanette's hands and looked deeply into her eyes. "I need this, Jean. Please."

"And if it doesn't…happen?"

"At least I would have tried. And eventually, I'll find someone else to scratch this itch."

"Well, all right then. Go get dressed." Jeanette stood as she spoke.

"Where are we going?"

"Shopping. We can't expect you to catch Malcolm Angel in those." Jeanette narrowed her eyes at Summer's pajamas.

"Don't you have to work?"

"It's a casting. On a Saturday. I'll have the agency send my book." Jeanette flitted her hands, gracefully dismissing Summer's concerns.

"That's the job to have…" Summer's eyes followed Jeanette as Jeanette made her way to the bedroom. "You don't feel like showing up so they send pictures of you."

"It's not quite that simple," Jeanette yelled from her closet. "And I've worked mighty long and hard to get to this point."

"I know that, Jean." Still clutching the picture, she

joined Jeanette in the closet. Summer watched Jeanette forage for clothes. "So don't throw it all away on me."

"Throw what away?" Jeanette held up a black tank top as she spoke. "My career?" Jeanette laughed. "No worries. This is way more exciting."

"What is? Seeing me finally let my passion lead my brain?"

"Well, that…" Jeanette tossed her head back and forth, weighing her answer. "And…"

"And, what?"

"Seeing Malcolm Angel finally get what's coming to him." Jeanette's gorgeous blue eyes sparkled. "This is more than your summer, Sum. If you actually succeed in having a purely physical relationship with Malcolm without getting your heart broken, well then, I'd say you would have single-handedly made one great step for womankind." Jeanette beamed. "Although, rumor has it you'll need a hell of a lot more than a single hand to manage the likes of him."

"Jeanette!" Summer felt the heat rise in her cheeks.

"Oh, relax." Suddenly, Jeanette fixed her eyes on Summer's face.

"What?" Summer reached up to see if she had any breakfast left on her chin.

Jeanette gazed left and right, considering her options. "I think we'll start with shopping and move on to hair."

"My hair?" Summer reached up and grabbed a lock of hair that was falling over her shoulder. She twirled it nervously. "What's wrong with my hair?"

"Nothing. Your hair is gorgeous. But what you do with it—"

"There's something wrong with ponytails?"

"No. Not when you're delivering a whole batch of puppies."

"Really?" Summer tapped her foot. "First of all, it's a litter. And second of all—"

Jeanette held up her hand. "Good grief. When it comes to going after Malcolm Angel, we may have to teach you a few basic conversation skills."

"Like what?" Summer crossed her arms.

"Like stop correcting people."

"Sorry."

"And if you're going to do that—" Jeanette mimed Summer's crossed arms, "then at least do it in a way that shows your cleavage."

"Jeanette…" Summer looked away.

"Summer…to catch him—this guy," Jeanette pointed to Malcolm's picture. "You're going to have to dumb it down and gloss it up a bit."

"You mean, pretend to be someone else entirely?"

"Well, yes."

Summer grinned. "That is exactly what I was hoping you were going to say."

****

Summer stared at herself in the salon mirror.

"Oh my goodness…" She leaned in for a better look.

"See?" Jeanette stood next to Summer's chair, beaming. "You are a goddess."

"Yeah?"

"Yeah." Jeanette put her hand on Summer's shoulder and squeezed.

"I've never looked like this before…" Summer turned her head to the right and left, staring at her smoky eyes and contoured cheeks. Her mouth was full and glossy. Summer was always okay with what she looked like—natural straw blonde hair, a little too coarse and free, hardly any makeup, and full lips that were their own cherry color, although usually damaged from her nervous tic of biting them. But until now, Summer never imagined she could play in the leagues with professional models.

"You're welcome." Chazz, Jeanette's hairstylist, waltzed up to them.

"My hair…" Summer stared in the mirror, transfixed. "It's so shiny and soft." She lifted a hand to touch her hair.

"No!" Jeanette and Chazz yelled in unison.

"You can't touch." Jeanette gently guided Summer's hand away.

"Not my masterpiece," Chazz reprimanded good-naturedly. "You are to go immediately home, slide into your outfit and head to the concert. How are you getting there?" Chazz turned to Jeanette.

"Elijah's sending a car."

"Good." Chazz nodded his approval. "Make sure you tell them you need it climate controlled—sixty-eight degrees."

"For my hair?" Summer faced them, flabbergasted.

"Yes." Chazz appraised Summer like she was the most pathetically naïve creature ever to walk into his salon. And she may very well be. "Hair has its own life. We must take care of straightened hair, treat it kindly. Don't expose it to rain or wind or…" he closed his eyes and shook his head solemnly, "humidity."

"Um," Summer looked at Chazz through the reflection in the mirror. "You do know hair is dead, right?"

Chazz patted her shoulder, condescendingly. "Not anymore, dear. Not anymore." Chazz turned to Jeanette and steepled his hands into prayer. "Namaste." Chazz bowed to them both and sashayed off.

Before she could stand, Chazz turned back and placed his hand aside his mouth, whispering. "And I want first dibs on the gossip. I created that—" he pointed at Summer. "I do not expect to read about Malcolm Angel's one night stand with the hot vet in some gossip magazine."

"You told him?" Summer glared at Jeanette.

"Shh…" Jeanette fanned her hands. "He did me a favor. He needed some kind of payment."

"I'm assuming he takes credit cards."

Jeanette placed her hands on Summer's shoulders, staring at her in the mirror. She smiled. "Sum, you couldn't afford him."

Summer frowned. "But Jean, I can't let you do this. You already bought me the outrageously expensive outfit. Who knew a pair of jeans could cost so much?"

Jeanette stood up straight, laughing. "Don't even think about the outfit. It's my pleasure, and it's a tax deduction for me."

"Really?"

"Um-hm."

"Told you, you have a head for business."

Jeanette spun Summer's chair around so they were facing one another. "Enough." Jeanette raised her eyebrows. "Look, Sum, if you're going to learn to play in this world, even for one night, you need to start thinking less practically. As of this moment, Dr. Summer Wynters, your brain is no longer in charge. Move your center down about a foot and a half and lead from there. 'Cause I can pretty much guarantee Malcolm's leading from a spot even farther south."

Summer covered her mouth with her hand, and they both giggled as they made their way from the salon.

Chapter Three

Summer fidgeted in her seat.

"Cool it," Jeanette whispered. "You're ruining the image."

"What image?"

"The cool one I have. Haven't you noticed everyone staring at you? They are all trying to figure out who you are. So for tonight, you are Malcolm Angel's girlfriend."

"Girlfriend—?"

"Oh, just go with it. To belong in this world, you need to act like you belong."

Summer adjusted the low cut drape on the front of her satin shirt. A spaghetti strap fell off her shoulder, and she slid it back on. "I'm freezing."

"That's the point. Not only do you look gorgeous, but your nipples will harden."

Summer's cheeks burned, making her eternally grateful it was dark in the auditorium. "Did you honestly just say that?"

"I most certainly did. You want to go to bed with the man who will be on that stage in ten minutes time…? Get in line. Because nearly every other woman in here wants it too."

Summer crossed and uncrossed her legs, her high heeled boots lifting into the empty space before her. They had perfect seats—directly in the front row.

Summer had never before sat in a seat like this, and she was amazed to find it waiting for her even though they had purposely arrived late and missed the warm-up bands. Jeanette led one glamorous life.

"I don't know what I was thinking." Summer shook her head as she looked around. Everywhere, seats were packed with gorgeous women, all after the same thing she was. She sunk down into herself. What was she thinking? That was the problem, she wasn't thinking. And that was always dangerous.

"Look to your left," Jeanette tossed her head. "But be discreet."

Summer turned to see seat after seat filled with beautiful women of all ages. All were in black, all wearing heavy makeup, and most had visible tattoos.

"I'm the only one who's not in black," Summer whispered to Jeanette.

"That will make you stand out."

"Guess we forgot my tattoo, huh?"

"Didn't forget. That's one of your biggest selling points. Nearly everyone here has a tattoo somewhere. It's become common. Done. You have virgin flesh."

"Virgin flesh?"

"Yup."

"That's a thing?" Summer suddenly wished she was buried in a lab coat, in the middle of a clinic somewhere.

"It is now." Jeanette turned in her seat to look at Summer. "The only way you'll have a chance tonight is by making yourself as different from everyone else as possible. Yes, we're going to say you're a model, but that's only to get your foot in the door. And because Malcolm Angel only ever—and I mean *ever*—dates models."

"No one will believe I'm a model, Jean." Summer looked down, her dreams deflating.

"They will tonight." Jeanette smiled smugly.

"Well, I'm glad this is only for one night, because any longer, and I'd never be able to keep up this façade. I don't know how you do this night after night."

"Have some fun with it." Jeanette squeezed Summer's hand. "For tonight you are a tall, gorgeous, jade-eyed model, new to the city, with virgin flesh."

Summer laughed out loud, covering her mouth. "I sound like a character in a young adult vampire novel."

Jeanette rolled her eyes and giggled along. Summer laughed even harder, leaning forward.

"Oh!" Summer's top slipped down, and she grabbed it just before her nipples were completely exposed. She covered her mouth with her hand, leaning against Jeanette, laughing until her sides hurt.

Summer tossed her head, a tear rolling down her cheek from the laughter. She took a deep breath, calming herself.

That's when she caught a glimpse of backstage, and saw Malcolm Angel in the wings, staring at her, smiling along with her laughter.

****

Malcolm was momentarily sidetracked by this woman sitting in the front row next to Jeanette, the girlfriend of his business manager, Elijah. There was something about her—beautiful, absolutely, but something else. She seemed so out of place, a feeling he understood completely, although he would never admit it to anyone. She also seemed above everything and everyone surrounding her, not in a conceited way, but in a real, honest way. She was, in a word, different. And that intrigued Malcolm.

"Mal?" It was his stage manager.

"Yeah?" Malcolm couldn't tear his eyes off this woman in the green top. She had looked away now, but Malcolm was certain, even from this distance, he had seen her blush. If that was true, what an incredibly welcomed change from the women who usually sat in the front row, licking their lips and baring their breasts on purpose. Malcolm laughed slightly, reliving the moment of this girl's top falling, of how embarrassed she seemed, of how it made her laugh.

"You okay?"

"Yeah." Malcolm chuckled, amazed at how very okay he was feeling all of a sudden.

The lights were dimming on the audience, but Malcolm stayed still, staring at her until the last glimmer had faded. That was it. After the show was over, he would find out who she was. Until then, well he was going to dazzle her with his show.

****

When Malcolm Angel glided onto the stage, the audience went wild. They had sat through three warm-up bands just waiting for Malcolm and his band, and they were impatient and hungry. Summer felt her heart rate increase, and her palms grow sweaty.

Jeanette eyed her coyly.

"It's a natural biological response to the primal plans I have scheduled for tonight."

"Uh-huh," Jeanette cooed, laughing. "Face it, Summer, he's incredibly hot."

Summer bit her lip and breathed deeply. There was no way to deny it. Malcolm Angel was incredibly sexy.

27

Malcolm wielded his microphone like a weapon, sauntering downstage—dangerously close to Summer. Summer sat back in her seat, inhaling sharply, and a cocky sideways grin spread across Malcolm's face. So it wasn't her imagination. He did notice her.

Malcolm turned back to his band, and Summer jumped with the heavy downbeat of the bass drum. Immediately Malcolm and his band broke into a new release that was already an international hit. As the music grew louder, Summer felt herself become swept up, swaying with the music. He was magical to watch. Yes, he was sexy and his voice sent chills down her spine, but he was also incredibly talented. And his music was inspiring. Summer didn't care what Jeanette had said, there was no way this man was dumb.

Summer sat glued to her seat, her breath racing, as once again, Malcolm made his way near to her. He was close enough that she could see the sweat glistening on his forehead, and her eyes spontaneously made their way up and down his body. He was thin, but not "rock star drug induced" skinny, and he appeared much taller and stronger in person. Summer was fighting to breathe now, inhaling audibly through her nose. After Malcolm sang another few verses of his song, he winked at her.

Summer sat up straight and smiled, feeling like a schoolgirl with a crush.

"We have contact," Jeanette whispered, leaning over.

Summer looked away to hide her blush, and over her shoulder she saw the angry stares from the other women in her row. She couldn't let herself care. It wasn't like they were on a marriage reality show, and Malcolm was choosing the woman he was planning to marry. Summer just wanted him for one night—this one night. And then from there, if his reputation was founded, there would be plenty of Malcolm to go around for all of them.

****

Malcolm was on fire tonight, and that wasn't necessarily a good thing. He knew judging his performance meant he was distanced from it, and to be distanced meant mediocrity. He had to live his show. His song finished, and he stopped short, holding his mic in the air over his head. Judging from the screams he heard, no one seemed to notice he was…somewhere else. He looked back at his band. Surely, Jimmy, his bass player, would tell him if he was blowing it. Nothing. Jimmy just smiled and started the next song. Malcolm exhaled. So it seems he could successfully focus on the blonde in the green shirt and put on a hell of a performance.

Go me, Malcolm thought, grinning.

Jeanette stood up, and the blonde followed. Standing next to Jeanette, the blonde wasn't quite as tall, but best Malcolm could guess, she was probably five nine or five ten. A model, no doubt. For a second Malcolm's face dropped from disappointment, and he couldn't understand why. He dated models all the time—frankly, it was what was expected of him. But this woman appeared different… Malcolm shook his head. He had no idea why he was having these thoughts—or any thoughts about her—while he was performing…or any other time.

Still not the slightest bit tired, Malcolm had sung, danced, and performed his way through almost the entire show, and it was time to slow things down. First you bring the audience's energy up, and then let the romance wash down over them. It was his formula and it worked, as long as he could continue to perform taxing ballads near the end of his shows. He could. He was blessed with a good voice, and he was well-trained, so he knew how to sing an entire show without causing the slightest bit of damage to his vocal chords. But still, most nights he would be tired by this point. For some reason, tonight, he had an abundance of extra energy.

Malcolm sat on the stool supplied for him and picked up his guitar. He was about to play the song that made every woman swoon, the song that easily made him the most beddable man in the business—a love song that no one, ever, truly understood.

And that made Malcolm incredibly sad.

Malcolm took a deep breath. He looked out at the audience, the people swaying in anticipation. They knew what was coming, the ballad most of America had used as a wedding song for nearly the past twenty years. The song more people had fallen in love to than any other song in history. At times, Malcolm would announce an engagement or a proposal before he started the song—the audience loving the interaction, everyone falling even more deeply in love with Malcolm's idea of love. If they only knew, Malcolm thought, shaking his head.

Just as he was about to play the first chord, Malcolm felt compelled to look over at her. She smiled sweetly, but the sincerity of her smile made Malcolm melancholic. He smiled back, a small, but real, smile. Then, somewhere deep inside, in the place Malcolm never allowed himself to go, in the place he had closed off all those years ago, something stirred.

"Hell no," Malcolm muttered, jumping to his feet. The crowd gasped in response. Most of them had been to as many of Malcolm's concerts as he had, and they knew the routine. If he sits with his acoustic guitar, then it's time for a love ballad. People shuffled and groaned, and silence began to sit heavily over the audience. Malcolm needed to fix this, fast.

Thinking on his feet, Malcolm walked to the edge of the stage and stared down at the girl in green. He saw her sit back farther into her seat, her hand resting on her tummy, her breath racing in and out of her chest—and what a chest. If those were real—damn. Malcolm signaled to security, and soon two very large men were standing next to the girl. Her already large eyes widened with anticipation. He liked that. It made him think about watching her eyes widen for other reasons…but no. Not now. Not in front of thousands of fans. Malcolm smiled at the girl, reassuringly, and picked up his mic.

"Hell no…I'm not gonna sing this song alone. Not when there's beauty like this around." The audience whooped in appreciation. Sure, some of the women would be jealous, but as soon as he opened his mouth, they'd forgive him, getting caught up in the romance of the situation.

Malcolm held out his hand to the girl, forcing a smile, swallowing his guilt. He knew he had made her a pawn in his elaborate game of subterfuge, but he had no choice. Everything Malcolm had was at stake here, and he couldn't blow it.

Malcolm raised his eyebrows as he looked down at the girl. He prayed she wouldn't leave him hanging. He exhaled quietly as she stood up and allowed herself to be escorted to the edge of the stage. She stood there, looking up at him, waiting for the next move…his next move… Malcolm inhaled deeply, nodding. He liked it. He liked the way she looked at him and how incredibly masculine he felt right now. He thrust his jaw forward and reached down for her hand. Her look of surprise when security lifted her up onto the stage was endearing. She was standing before him now, even more gorgeous up close, but looking completely lost and uncomfortable. Malcolm wanted to make it right.

"What's your name?" Malcolm asked, holding out his mic.

The girl didn't answer. Malcolm smiled his trademark cocky smile, but she looked even more terrified. Her breathing grew faster, making her incredibly voluptuous top rise up and down. She looked over her shoulder at Jeanette, and Malcolm felt a punch to his gut. He couldn't leave her hanging. He needed to make this right.

As she turned back to him, Malcolm covered his mic with his hand and leaned forward. He felt her catch her breath as he brushed against her shoulder slightly. He inhaled—she smelled clean but full of promise, like Manhattan at dawn.

"I promise…" Malcolm whispered, "I won't let anything bad happen to you."

****

Summer stood up straight, inhaling again without ever remembering to exhale. His words—contrived, practiced, and fake as they were, were nonetheless a pure aphrodisiac to Summer. She smiled then, a real, honest smile—an odd response to such insincere words, but there it was. He smiled back…a smile that hit her deep in her belly, and made her feel like she was the only woman in the world. And there, onstage, in front of thousands of Malcolm's screaming fans, Summer finally understood Jeanette's warnings. She didn't believe in love, but Summer couldn't deny this crazy, primordial attraction that could, if she wasn't careful... really...really...hurt.

"What's your name?" he asked again, his eyes bright, his smile wide. It was obvious he was having fun with her situation, but he appeared good-natured, and not at all malicious.

Summer stared at him, lost in his dark eyes and the grooves on either side of his mouth, lining his cheeks. He looked—dangerous. And sexy as hell. Summer shook her head, trying to concentrate, and trying desperately to remember her name.

"Summer..." There. She exhaled. She'd remembered. She just prayed the day would never come when Malcolm Angel would show up in her operating room, or she wouldn't remember an osteotome from a bone ronguer.

"Summer..."

The way her name rolled off his tongue made her long for him to say it again and again.

"I think summer has just become my favorite season."

The audience hollered in appreciation.

Malcolm reached out and gave her warm hand a tiny squeeze. He headed back to his stool and picked up his guitar. Summer stood there, staring at him, waiting, in vain, for her instincts to finally kick in. If only she knew what to do...

It didn't matter. Once Malcolm Angel played his

first chord, she, and every other person in that coliseum, was lost. He finally looked away from her, and down at his guitar. Summer relaxed and gave over to Malcolm and his music, confident no one in the audience was looking at her.

Summer listened to the song she had heard a million times before—but somehow, in this giant venue before all of these people, it sounded incredibly intimate. It also sounded…different. She cocked her head, watching him, listening as he poured out his pain for thousands of people, and she wondered, for the first time since she paid any attention to Malcolm Angel, if his pain may be real. His lyrics: "This time I'll know—not to let you go—before we ever get a chance…," smooth. His words: "Forever," "Baby," "Stay with me…," intoxicating.

Summer closed her eyes, letting herself get swept away—and why not? Wasn't this what she was here for?

All too soon the song ended. Summer opened her eyes, and her gaze landed on Malcolm, staring at her. Without ever tearing his eyes from hers, he stood and walked to her. There, in front of thousands of people, Malcolm reached out, took her hand, lifted it to his lips, and kissed it.

Summer smirked at him, understanding she was part of his elaborate show, but not caring in the least. He grinned back and once again, he covered his mic. He leaned forward to whisper into her ear.

"Wait for me later?"

Summer felt her body tremble in response as she nodded. He smiled sweetly, and then hummed into her ear once again.

"Stay with Jeanette. Backstage. I'll find you when all the craziness is over."

"That would be a great song lyric," Summer blurted. She closed her eyes and bit her lip. How could she be so stupid? She might as well tell Michelangelo what to paint.

"Yeah?" He raised his eyebrows in response. "Maybe it would."

A small smile turned up the corners of his lips, and Summer smiled back, feeling her heart perform a fairly common occurrence that was entirely new to her. It was easily explained in layman's terms as the moment one's heart has a palpitation, or a tiny hiccup in its rhythm, that can be manifested by stress—stress such as standing onstage in the middle of Madison Square Garden with thousands of people staring at you—or, in other words…Malcolm's smile made Summer's heart skip a beat.

Chapter Four

From backstage, Summer watched the chaos unfurl around her. People ran back and forth pushing equipment and moving props. She was stunned Malcolm's job—which appeared worlds apart from hers in every way—was actually not so very different. Behind the scenes, Malcolm had the same hustle and bustle going that Summer encountered when pet owners, ranchers, or farmers frantically described symptoms Summer couldn't immediately detect. But in the operating room, like on the stage, there was the sanctity of peace, as she, like Malcolm, concentrated only on the job at hand. Huh.

Jeanette walked up and bumped Summer on the shoulder. "Told ya that shirt was a good choice."

"Jean," Summer hugged her. "Did I look like an idiot? Honestly."

"I would say not. Actually, you looked like the woman every woman here wished she were."

"I don't know about that…" Summer felt the heat in her cheeks as she looked out at Malcolm.

"Is that me making you blush? Or him?"

Jeanette had to raise her voice to be heard, and Summer hushed her.

"For goodness sake. I'm not blushing."

"Okayyyy…." Jeanette smiled and took Summer by the hand. She turned Summer to face her.

"I know that look, Jean." Summer rolled her eyes.

"Look, you're a grown-up. A high achieving, ass-kicking grown-up."

Summer sighed, exasperated.

"But this may be your last chance to say no."

"I can always say no, Jean. This is the United States of America, and if I say no—"

"Yes, yes." Jeanette waved Summer off. "What I mean is, once Malcolm Angel sets his sights on you, I've never known a woman who could say no."

"His eyes are...something..." Summer let her gaze fall back toward Malcolm.

Malcolm turned just then and caught a glimpse of her. He smiled.

"Well, I see my work here is done." Jeanette threw her bag over her shoulder.

"You're leaving?" Summer's heartbeat raced again as panic set in.

"Going to catch a late dinner with Elijah, and then we'll be staying in the same hotel as the band. The same hotel you'll be in, I guess."

Jeanette raised her eyebrows, and Summer smirked.

"Wait..." Summer narrowed her eyes. "If you all live in New York City, why do you stay in a hotel after a performance?"

Jeanette tipped her head in a way that would have been condescending had it come from anyone else. But Summer knew, coming from Jeanette, it was a gesture filled with concern. "No one wants to go home straight after a performance. This way it...keeps the party going."

"Huh." Summer nodded, understanding. So

Malcolm Angel never took women back to his own apartment. Made sense, really.

"So let me explain how this will work." Jeanette furrowed her brow as she spoke. "A security guard will check your ID."

"My ID?" Summer recoiled in surprise. "I'm clearly over twenty-one."

"They don't take chances with the likes of Malcolm Angel, Sum. And they're not checking if you're old enough to drink. Get it?"

Summer nodded, breathing deeply. What kind of life was this man living? For a moment, a flicker of time, Summer felt bad for him.

"Summer. Pay attention." Jeanette glanced at her watch. "They'll drop you off at Malcolm's hotel room to wait for him. You'll have dinner when he arrives."

"Wait…dinner. Will it be a deal that I'm a vegetarian?"

"The man dates models. You'll have the least convoluted diet restrictions of any woman he's ever eaten with. I promise."

Summer nodded, feeling a tad insecure at the thought of following in the bed sheets of women who looked like Jeanette.

"Anyway, you'll have dinner in the room—"

"In the room? Isn't that a bit… too…normal for a rock star? I imagined—"

"Sum," Jeanette placed her hand on Summer's arm. "You couldn't even begin to imagine what this hotel is like. You've never seen anything like it. His suite is half the top floor, and it has a bunch of separate rooms, including a dining room. Anyway, when it's time…you'll make your way to the lounge for drinks, or go straight to the bedroom."

Summer placed her hands on her cheeks, cooling her blush.

"If at any time you decide you're through, you know where to find me." Jeanette grabbed her cell and texted Summer her room number. Jeanette's eyes fell heavy on Summer. "If you do this, he will kick you out when he's done. Understand this, Sum."

"I got it," Summer whispered, looking at Malcolm out of the corner of her eye.

"He's got a reputation of being a shit, but not until the woman's gone and can't cause him any trouble. So while you're there, he'll be a gentleman. When he's done, he'll say he has an early call time tomorrow which is bullshit, but so is everything else in this life." Jeanette sighed. "He'll walk you to his hotel room door, and someone will usher you down to his car." Jeanette took Summer by the shoulders and stared into her eyes. "And he will never think of you again. You sure you're okay with that?"

"Jean…" Summer reached up and removed Jeanette's hands. "I want irreverence. Not manners."

Jeanette nodded. "Head back to the apartment, and I'll meet up with you tomorrow for all the details. Capiche?"

"Yup." Summer nodded, sneaking another peek at Malcolm.

Jeanette kissed Summer on the cheek, then pulled back, studying her. "Above all, have fun, Sum."

Summer broke out into a mischievous smile. "I intend to."

****

Summer barely had time to find her way to a

bathroom in Malcolm's hotel suite before he arrived. She felt him walk in before she ever saw him—his electrical aura preceding him, sending shockwaves through her body.

He made a surprising entrance. She was expecting Malcolm to crash through the door, security paving his way, while groupies threw themselves against him. Instead, her heart fluttered when he walked through the door alone. His discreet and unassuming entrance almost made this feel normal. Almost.

"Summer…" Again her name rolled off his tongue. He smiled from across the room.

Summer let her eyes make their way to him. He was dressed in a black button down shirt, sleeves rolled up—exposing incredibly strong forearms—dark jeans, and dress shoes. When he lifted his arm to run his hand through his hair, her mouth dropped open. He was lean, hungry, sexy, and dangerous. Summer bit her lip, energy swirling below her belly.

"Hello, Malcolm." She had no idea what to do with herself. Nerves were coursing through her at unprecedented speeds. She wrung her hands, dropping them when he looked at her. Still nervous, she tried shaking them. He smirked, and Summer froze. She glued her arms to her sides, not wanting to look like a fledgling bird trying to take flight.

"I'm glad you stayed to have dinner with me. I wasn't sure when I saw the look on your face onstage…" He shook his head, chuckling, and made his way around the room, landing at the bar.

"I—I'm not accustomed to that many eyes on me." Summer didn't recognize her voice. It was low and breathy.

"Really?" He raised his eyebrows. "I would have thought models were used to the attention."

"Oh, um..." So Jeanette had already told him Summer was a model. Now all she had to do was to pull it off. Absentmindedly, Summer reached up and ran a hand through her hair. She suddenly remembered the straightening and blowout and pulled her hand away, fast. "I do mostly print..." Summer shook her head. She hated lying.

"Got it." His eyes ran up and down her body as he held up a bottle of champagne.

Summer began to fidget, shifting from one high heeled boot to the other. Malcolm was most definitely sizing her up. How long would it be before he guessed that squeezed in under Jeanette's custom creation was a woman who was most certainly not a model...?

"Champagne?"

"Um, sure." Why the heck not? He hadn't thrown her out yet, and this was her one night. Her kickoff to a summer to remember. As the years go by, and she's working in her clinic in a small country town, she will never have to wonder, "what if." How many people can say that?

"Good."

Malcolm popped the cork easily, and Summer allowed herself to discreetly gawk at his exposed forearm muscles. Her breath grew shallower with every move he made. He poured her a glass and walked to her with it. His proximity made her head pound, and she stepped back, suddenly dizzy.

Merely the otolithic organs in my vestibular system, sending the wrong signal to my brain... Rationalizing her feelings made her feel momentarily better.

Then he looked at her, the deep groves in his face framing his perfectly white, amazing smile, and Summer's heart began a mad dash toward a finish line she hoped she wouldn't see for hours...

It was merely a biological reaction. Fight or flight. She was nervous, so her adrenaline pumped faster, causing an increase in blood pressure and heart rate. Summer shook her head. Oh, the heck with it. It was him—Malcolm Angel. He was hot as hell. The intensity of his eyes sent a charge through her.

Summer returned Malcolm's smile, vowing to let her body take over, and for once, to keep her analytical mind at bay. She exhaled, noticing he was carrying only one glass of champagne.

"Thank you." She took the glass from him. "You don't drink?"

****

It was the way she asked the question. He'd never been asked like that before. And it was sooner than anyone else had ever asked—it took most women two or three glasses themselves before they realized he wasn't drinking with them. "You don't drink?" was very different from, "You're not drinking?" Maybe he was reading too much into a few meaningless words. Maybe she just spoke off the cuff...but something about this woman made him think she was rarely frivolous...in thought or in life.

"Quick pick up." Malcolm nodded his head to her. He thought about his usual response to a question like that, "No, baby, I wanna be here with you, completely." Of course it was cheesy and insincere, but it did the job. Most women ate those words up. But once again,

Malcolm had this annoying feeling that Summer wasn't most women.

"I don't have to drink, either." Summer placed the glass down on a nearby table and smiled at him.

Her look was resolute. She was strong—he could tell. She was a fighter, or had fought her way through something. Malcolm always recognized this look in others and appreciated it. She looked like the type who would do whatever she had to, to get the job done, and right now, it was to make sure Malcolm Angel wasn't tempted by alcohol. Malcolm smiled, there was no way she could know alcohol was the one vice that temped him the least.

"No, no…" Malcolm picked up her glass and handed it back to her. "It's not that I can't, it's that I choose not to. Sometimes." He added the "sometimes" in case their encounter made its way to the gossip papers. He had no interest in people learning anything about the real him—like the fact that he hadn't touched a drop of alcohol in nearly twenty years.

"Oh, okay." She held onto her glass again and sipped.

Malcolm studied her, more intrigued than usual. He felt like this woman, a total stranger, somehow deserved more. But more was impossible for him to give. He stared into her giant green eyes. Surely he could try something. "But uh…thank you." He looked away immediately, not trusting himself to connect on any real human level.

"You're welcome."

Her voice was sweet, and her eyes held his longer than he meant.

"But," she added, taking another sip, "if you ever

do decide you want some champagne, this is the one to drink. I've never tasted anything like it."

She smiled happily, tossing her head, and Malcolm smiled along with her.

****

Summer picked at her dinner of artichoke soup and parmesan crusted gnocchi. The food was delicious, and Jeanette was right, asking to eat vegetarian was an easy request. Malcolm ordered like he had ordered vegetarian a million times before. And probably had. Summer stabbed a gnocchi with a shaking hand, unable to deny her nerves.

They were sitting across from each other at a small bistro-like table. The dining room was modern and sleek, like the rest of the hotel room, but the feel of their dinner was intimate.

Malcolm looked over at her nearly untouched dinner and knit his brow. "Don't like it?" He nodded to her plate. "'Cause I can order something else…"

He was nearly out of his seat when Summer stopped him. "No, Malcolm, please. The food is delicious." His eyes landed on hers, and she looked away. He was handsome, undeniably, but there was so much more. His face was drawn and ragged making him look dangerous, and his presence filled the vastness of the suite. She ventured a peek into his eyes…they were dark, soulful and hungry, but filled with something unexplainable. He was every bit as primal as the animals she cared for daily. Jeanette was right, there was no way Summer would ever be able to say no.

"Oh…" He nodded. "I get it. Models don't eat." He raised his eyebrows and shoveled in another bite.

"No…" Summer shook her head. "It's not that at

all." She shifted in her seat, uncomfortable over the lie she was lamely trying to perpetuate. "I normally eat…a lot." She giggled and placed her hand to her mouth. This second glass of champagne was making her giddy.

"Then what's up?" Malcolm smiled along, looking sincerely interested.

"Honestly…?" Summer pushed herself back from the table. She cringed with the word, "honestly." "The truth is…" She wanted to tell him the truth, but he would kick her out for sure. Jeanette warned her of that. Then what would she have? "The truth is, I'm nervous." She exhaled. At least she was able to express one real truth, and it felt like such a relief.

"Why?" Malcolm asked, pushing his plate away.

"Honestly?" Darn. There was that word again. She wanted to kick herself.

"Please." Malcolm rested his elbows on the table, crossing his arms.

Summer inhaled his incredibly masculine scent from all the way across the table. She stared at his tired but sexy face, his body that was lean, and strong. She looked around his hotel suite that probably cost more for one night than her tuition for one semester; a room that rivaled her wildest notion of a palace.

"Malcolm…" She tilted her head, hoping he would fill in the rest.

"Yes?"

"Oh, for heaven's sake." Summer stood up, laughing. "In case you've forgotten, let me remind you, you're Malcolm Angel."

He leaned back in his chair, his face betraying just the slightest glimmer of disappointment.

"Oh, I'm sorry…" Summer walked to him and

placed a hand on his shoulder.

He looked up then, his eyes blazing with passion, and she pulled her hand away immediately.

"I'm not particularly good with people." Summer shrugged, moving back from him, her nerves on edge. "I didn't mean you were such an intimidating force merely because of your name and persona…it's also because of you. Just you." Summer shook her head, daring to say something she normally wouldn't. "Blame my inhibitions and free flowing rhetoric on the champagne or the fact that we're total strangers who will never see each other again—" At her last words, Summer was certain she saw him flinch. She pushed on. "But even if you weren't Malcolm Angel rock star, you'd still be intimidating and awe-inspiring, just as yourself…as a…a man."

Summer felt her whole body grow incredibly warm. "I'm sorry," she muttered, looking down. "That was foolish. I don't know what got into me. I told you I was terrible with people…"

Malcolm looked away but reached out and grabbed her hand in a way that made her jump. She placed her free hand on her chest, feeling her heart race. His hand held hers, and in his grasp, Summer was certain she felt all the words he would never speak.

Chapter Five

Malcolm wondered, as he tightened his grasp on her hand, if she could ever possibly understand this is the closest he had been to another human being in nearly twenty years.

He shook his head, laughing at himself. Sure, she was slightly tipsy, what was his excuse for these free flowing feelings? Malcolm looked at Summer and saw the concern etched into her forehead. The last thing he wanted was for her to feel stupid. Yes, it's true two glasses of champagne were probably enough to do her in...but still, her words were heartfelt, and they were intended to make him feel better.

Still clutching her hand, Malcolm stood. She shied away slightly, and her hair brushed against his shoulder. He liked it. Their bodies were close now, and it was surely the time he would have led any woman into his bedroom. He knew he should lead Summer there as well—it's what she was expecting and what he wanted, ever since he caught that first glimpse of her from stage. But tonight, he felt different. The way she smiled at him onstage, the honesty in her eyes...something felt...altered tonight. He breathed in deeply. Maybe it wasn't her at all; maybe it was the beginning of the summer season that made him feel this way...

She slipped her warm hand from his grasp, and Malcolm stepped back from her. Running his eyes up and down her body, he loved what he saw—her incredibly full breasts, the curves on her hips and backside…she was beautiful. She had a type of body Malcolm hadn't seen in all the years of dating models—the type of body he, and most men, loved—thin, but with definite rounded turns.

Malcolm had become proficient at pretending to be attracted to the bodies of the women he dated. They were beautiful, no doubt, and like a work of cold, modern art, they could be appreciated for their own style of perfection: tall, stick skinny, hard, and angular. But this body before him…Summer's body… He shifted his weight from foot to foot, fighting his growing attraction, amazed at how easy it was to be tempted by her softness and swell. Even though she was trying to hide it under her blossoming shirt, Malcolm loved the way her tummy was slightly rounded—convex instead of concave—and he wondered why she felt the need to disguise it. Probably because she, like he, was fed unreal images of what a female body should look like. Malcolm wondered why no one in the fashion business ever dressed bodies like Summer's. This body would inspire Malcolm to buy something for the woman he cared about…if there was a woman he cared about.

Malcolm smiled at the thought of Summer's body, knowing full well he was being had. There was no way a woman with this much body fullness was a model, but he wasn't going to say anything, just in case she hadn't realized it yet. If Summer had come to the city to pursue her dreams of being a model, well, life would squash those dreams soon enough, without his help.

"Can I help you?" She caught his stare.

She smiled in the most relaxed, unassuming way, and it made Malcolm happy.

"Well actually…" Malcolm stepped closer to her and at once, felt both her excitement and her hesitation.

Summer stepped back, distancing herself a bit so she was just out of his grasp. "What do you say you show me around this place?"

"The hotel room?" Malcolm raised his eyebrows.

"Yes. I've never seen a hotel room like this." She stopped and furrowed her brow. "Unless, are you too tired? I'm being insensitive. Sorry. You must be exhausted."

Once again this woman caught him by complete surprise. No one ever thought about how he was feeling. Of course he wasn't complaining or looking for sympathy. He was a musician, a rock star, with houses and cars and tons of money. He had everything—well, on the surface anyway, which was still a lot more than most people. But it just struck Malcolm that although he was constantly being criticized for using women, they were using him just the same.

"No," Malcolm shook his head. "Thanks, though. My adrenaline's still up. I won't get tired for quite some time." He fixed his stare on her.

Summer smiled coyly, and Malcolm wondered if she caught his meaning. Of course she did. This was not a woman who missed much of anything. He breathed her in, her scent now reminding him of a lazy summer day.

"So, the tour…" Walking beside her, Malcolm led Summer through the maze of rooms making up his hotel suite. "This is the sitting area, with a large screen TV…"

"Mm-hm…" Summer stared at all the high end, ultra modern furnishings. "Good grief," she turned and pointed to the corner of the living area, "is that a spiral staircase leading to another room of this suite?"

"The bedroom." Malcolm's gaze was heavy on hers, looking for the answer. He knew why she was here, but he still needed to be completely sure. He couldn't deny the attraction between them, but he had to be sure she wasn't expecting this to be the beginning of something he couldn't offer.

"Oh…"

Summer looked down, and Malcolm smiled at her blush.

"C'mon." Malcolm walked her through the rest of the suite, with stainless appliances and granite in the kitchen, and a balcony overlooking Manhattan.

"Wow," Summer whispered when she stepped out onto the balcony.

"Beautiful, huh?"

They were side by side, facing out over Manhattan.

"I never knew it could be this beautiful…"

"Are you new to the city?" Malcolm turned to her. He could feel her sensuality. He rested his forearms on the railing, noticing her stare.

"Been here for just a few days, actually."

She looked down as if she was embarrassed by this omission. The expression, "Just fell off the turnip truck" jumped to Malcolm's mind. He smiled.

"I'm just here for the summer." Summer shifted from foot to foot.

Malcolm wondered if her feet were getting tired in her high-heeled boots. How do women spend hours in those things?

"Really?" Malcolm knew if she were here to model, she would be giving it at least a year. And if she really wanted it, she would chase it indefinitely. No one can pursue a life dream with a clock for a master. Hell, when Malcolm was first starting out, he would have chased music forever if that's what it took. Nothing would have stopped him—no, nothing did stop him. Malcolm closed his eyes, halting his thoughts. He took a deep breath, shaking off a chill. Why? Why was he so melancholic tonight?

"Really." Summer turned to him.

Malcolm nodded. To her credit, she fixed her stare on him and offered no more explanation. She was playing some sort of game here. He just didn't know what it was. That didn't really surprise him; people, women, were usually with him because they were after something. The difference is, he always knew what they wanted. But with Summer, it was different.

Malcolm stepped closer to her and raised his hand. He reached out and touched her hair, letting his hand run down a long, shiny lock, wondering what she looked like straight out of a shower, without Jeanette's obvious input. He chuckled slightly at his surprising thoughts.

Summer closed her eyes and leaned against his hand. He flinched, the intimacy of the action scaring him… He always made sure any woman he was with understood his rules—this was one night only. He had no room or desire for a woman in his life. His life was perfectly bearable exactly as it was, and he wasn't about to risk it.

He pulled his hand back, but she grabbed it and returned it to her cheek. "I understand, Malcolm. I'm not an idiot."

She looked up at him with giant jade colored eyes, her lids, heavy. Malcolm shifted, making room in his jeans for his obvious attraction.

"Summer…"

"Shh…"

As he dropped his hand, she placed hers on his chest. Even through his shirt, Malcolm felt the warmth of her touch.

"I understand the rules. Jeanette explained them to me. I'm okay with it. You're not leading me on. Please don't feel any…concern about being with me. I mean, if you do want to be with me…"

She blushed again, looking down. Instinctually, Malcolm placed his finger under her chin and raised her giant, gorgeous eyes back up to his. Her slight insecurity riled a protective instinct Malcolm hadn't felt…maybe ever. As his eyes danced back and forth across hers, his body assured him he liked the pace this was going. He liked how she expected him to be a man. So many women made their way into his hotel room only to take charge from beginning to end. It was another thing society was feeding women—this idea they had to be wild, forward, and aggressive in the bedroom. Time after time, Malcolm would pop a champagne cork, only to turn back to the couch to find the woman fully naked, lying prone on his couch. Other times, women would climb on top of him in the elevator—whether they were alone or not. So often the women would be drunk, and that wasn't cool. Malcolm wouldn't do anything with a drunk. But a tad tipsy and fully coherent, like Summer, well that was just endearing. And he liked that she was waiting for him to make the moves. That she expected him to be a man. That she wanted him to work for her. He smiled.

"Hey," Malcolm whispered.

Summer stared at him, her eyes hungry.

"I wouldn't be here if I didn't wanna spend some time with you."

Summer exhaled and smiled, a real radiant smile that warmed Malcolm's heart. He liked her smile— warm, friendly, with perfect white teeth and pink lips. It made him feel happy. He let his hand come to rest on her cheek once more.

****

Summer could barely stand up. She loved the feeling of Malcolm's hand on her cheek. It was so incredibly intimate it awakened feelings in her she had never before experienced—of being wanted and desired and coveted. She liked feeling this close to Malcolm, she liked the strength of his arm, the sinews of his muscles, his wrist and forearm flexors, the brachloradialis...oh the heck with it, he oozed confidence, and that made him incredibly sexy.

She inhaled deeply, but as much as she was enjoying every second of this, she felt pressure. There was the definite element of time working against her. Hadn't Jeanette told her Malcolm would use her quickly and toss her out? Was she blowing this by spending too much time acting as if this was a normal date? And what was normal anyway? Did she actually know? The amount of sexual experience Summer had was severely limited. She had lost her virginity in the back of a pickup truck to a boy she dated in high school. The most memorable part of that experience was when it was over—lying there, staring up at the night sky, sipping a warm beer. After that, her next and only real experience was with Dr. Brad…and that was less than fulfilling.

But with Malcolm…her hands were tingling, and her whole body was alive with anticipation. He stroked her cheek, his thumb gently caressing her skin, and her breath raced. She closed her eyes and turned her head, her lips gently grazing his thumb. Summer looked up and saw desire in Malcolm—his chest heaving up and down. He stepped forward, his fingers gently tracing the outline of her lips. She wished she knew what to do, she was certain he dealt with incredibly sexy, knowledgeable women night after night…and here she was, waiting for him to make the moves. She knew, no matter what Malcolm did, it would most certainly fulfill her wildest fantasies…but would she fulfill his?

Malcolm stepped closer to her, and the warmth of the hot Manhattan night enveloped them. Summer felt a bead of perspiration trickle down between her breasts and her nipples harden. Malcolm's eyes dropped down to her breasts before he stepped even closer, their bodies full against one another. Summer could feel the leanness of his muscles as he pushed against her. She fit against him perfectly, her softness surrounded and protected by his strength. Her breasts pushed against his chest, and he wrapped his arms around her, letting his hands drop down to her backside. He moved his hands to her hips and pulled her even closer. Her breath hitched as she felt him against her…ready for her.

"Summer…"

A chill washed over Summer, eliciting tiny bumps up and down her arms. His voice was pure magic, and although it was a voice she knew well, she was hearing it for the first time tonight.

He leaned down, and Summer felt the slightest scruff from his unshaven chin brush against her cheek. She nuzzled against it, loving the feel of him—strong, and so incredibly masculine. She gripped his waist, steadying herself, her body aching…she wanted to give him everything—now. Her eyes floated up to meet his, and she was lost in the danger of his face, and the depth of his eyes.

His breath quickened, and she knew he was as invested as she was. His arms slid around her waist, and he held her, close.

Summer closed her eyes and stretched up onto her tiptoes. Her hands rested on his shoulders, grasping the material of his shirt. Malcolm leaned down, his lips nearly brushing hers…

Her breath ran away from her, and she closed her eyes, hoping her body would remember to keep up. But the heck with ventilation, diaphragmatic respiration, who cares? She was in Malcolm Angel's arms and he was about to…

She felt the warmth of his breath…his lips grazing hers, when she heard…

"Knock, knock. There you are."

Chapter Six

Summer jumped and broke apart from Malcolm. A slight gasp escaped as her cheeks burned with color. "It's only vascular dilation, brought about by stress," she muttered under her breath, but her attempts to calm down by using medical justifications and excuses were futile.

A strange man glanced at her—did she recognize him? Either way, he never bothered to lift his gaze high enough to make eye contact. Summer draped her arm across her hard and extremely noticeable nipples, cursing Jeanette under her breath.

Malcolm stuffed one hand into his pocket and stepped forward, offering his free hand to the man. After the men shook hands, Malcolm turned to Summer.

"Uh, Summer, this is my bass player, Jimmy."

"Hello." Of course…the bass player. He looked different offstage. Normal. Summer spoke as casually as she could, considering there was now a second man in this equation.

Jimmy said nothing but let his eyes run up and down Summer's body. Summer shook her head and glared at Malcolm. To his credit, Malcolm seemed embarrassed.

"Oh, uh, hi," Jimmy finally offered, stepping toward Summer.

Suddenly, Summer didn't feel right.

She put both hands behind her and grasped the rail of the balcony. Her grip tightened as she looked from man to man, wondering if her night of ecstasy was quickly becoming a night from hell. She glanced over her shoulder, preparing for an escape route, but there was no way down—they were just too high up. That meant she would have to get past both men to escape out the door. And there was no way she'd be able to outrun or fight off Malcolm.

Summer stood there seconds more, mentally kicking herself. Why? Why was someone as smart as she, acting so incredibly dumb? Because she was desperate? Because he was a celebrity? She scoffed. No matter who he was or wasn't, she'd allowed herself to go to a hotel room with a complete stranger. She shook her head. When did she become so careless? Time and again she had warned Jeanette against doing this exact thing, yet here Summer was. But Jeanette...surely Jeanette would know if Malcolm Angel was into some weird, kinky...anything...and would have warned her. Right?

Summer set her jaw and steeled her nerves. The one thing she was certain of is that she could rely on her brain. She was smart, and that would surely get her out of a jam. Just as she was about to speak, Jimmy turned to Malcolm.

"Any leftovers?" Jimmy tossed his head in the direction of Summer.

Malcolm shook his head.

Summer saw red. Her shoulders climbed up and rage took over where passion was, only moments before. "Any leftovers? Leftovers?" Her breathing quickened for an entirely different reason. "Seriously?" Summer glared at Malcolm, and all the desire she felt only minutes earlier, melted away. "That's what you think of women? I know you have no respect for us at all, but to pass us along when you're done? Handing your band members some poor unsuspecting woman when you're through with her?" Summer stepped closer to both men, hardly able to keep from yelling. She stood toe to toe with Malcolm, sadness replacing the anger she felt only seconds before. "It's my decision to be here with you. I'm a big girl. I knew there wasn't any romance here. I knew you…you…" she racked her brain for a word coarse enough, "…*used* women for one night only, and I was okay with that. But to pass us along like something you sell on eBay? 'Here you go guys, ready for the highest bidder…still warm from Malcolm Angel's bed'…" Summer shook her head, her stomach aching. "It's sickening, and you should be better than that."

With that, Summer grabbed her bag and stormed out of Malcolm's hotel room. She felt his eyes on her as she left.

****

"I don't want to talk about it." Summer marched past Jeanette, making her way into Jeanette's hotel room.

"It didn't go the way you'd hoped, I'm guessing." Jeanette was still dressed from the show with a wineglass in her hand. "I'm sorry, Sum."

Summer clomped around the room, wild with anger. Then it dawned on her. "Where's Elijah?"

"Meeting." Jeanette plopped down on the couch, pushing a fashion magazine out of the way.

58

Summer reasoned from the half full bottle of wine, Jeanette must have been alone all evening.

"I'm sorry, Jean." Summer softened, concentrating on her friend's unhappiness.

"Don't be. You sure you don't want to talk about it?"

"Ugh. Yes. I'm sure. Can I take a shower? I'll be quick. I want to get as far away from 'the woman who almost seduced Malcolm Angel' as possible."

"Almost, huh?"

Jeanette raised an eyebrow, and Summer crossed her arms in front of her chest. Jeanette chuckled.

"Of course. Take a shower. Feel better." Jeanette pointed behind Summer. "In there."

"Thanks. I promise to be gone before Elijah gets back."

"Don't worry about it." Jeanette swirled the wine in her glass before swallowing another big gulp. "He'll be too tired to do anything when he gets here anyway."

Jeanette shrugged, and Summer saw disappointment in her friend's gorgeous face.

"Jean, do you want to talk?"

"About as much as you do." Jeanette lifted her glass. "Come on, shower. I miss the real Summer. Then come sit with me, and we'll get loaded."

"Sounds like a plan." Summer exited to the bathroom.

****

Summer came out of the bathroom with her face scrubbed clean, and her hair back to its usual coarse, wavy self. Still grumpy, she walked into Jeanette's living room, planning to drown her sorrows.

Malcolm Angel was standing there.

"I—uh…" Unable to form words, Summer focused on cinching the belt of her white fluffy robe.

Malcolm stared at her as if she were a diamond on display in the window of a fancy New York jewelry store…and she didn't mind the feeling.

"You're beautiful," he blurted.

Startled, both women turned to him. Malcolm dragged his hand across his chin, seeming equally as surprised by his outburst.

He shook his head like he was fighting his way through a lingering fog. "I'm sorry. I just—you were beautiful before, but now you're just…gorgeous."

Malcolm stared at Summer in a way that unnerved her. The tiniest smirk turned up the corner of her lips, but she fought it away. She was too angry for insincere compliments. Malcolm stood straight, squaring his shoulders. Summer couldn't help but notice how tall he was, especially now she was out of those ridiculous boots.

Summer matched his posture, cinching her belt tighter. "If you're here to apologize—"

"I'm not."

"Excuse me?" Again, Summer began to get riled.

"I'm not here to apologize. But I'm willing to wait for your apology."

"What?" Summer felt herself flush. Was he insane?

"Oh boy…" Jeanette turned away. "Well, uh, if anyone needs me, I'll be in the bedroom."

"Why would I apologize to you?" Summer took a step forward, her chest heaving from anger.

"Because you were wrong." He raised an eyebrow.

"I was wrong?" Summer scoffed and turned away. "The only time I was wrong was in thinking there might be some decency in you."

Malcolm looked down at the ground and then back up to her. Summer stared into his eyes that were filled with pain. She felt herself soften.

"Yes..." Malcolm stuffed his hands into his pockets. "That part you were right about." His voice was soft and filled with agony. "There is no decency in me."

Summer chewed her lip. She was angry, but still, she ached for him. She hated to see any creature—person or animal—suffering.

"But you were wrong in your assumption." His eyes never veered from hers.

"How?" Summer crossed her arms in front of her chest, speaking through her clenched jaw.

"The leftovers...?"

"Don't remind me."

Summer began to walk off, but Malcolm lurched forward and grabbed her by the arm. She spun around, fuming, her face inches from his. She was angry, but heaven help her...

"If you would just wait a second..." His breath was warm on her face.

Summer fought to control her breathing. She looked at her arm, and Malcolm let go. She adjusted her robe.

"As I was saying." He cleared his throat. "The 'leftovers' Jimmy was looking for were from dinner."

Summer laughed. "Do you think I'm an idiot?"

"No, actually. Not in the least. But you—"

"You expect me to believe that the lead singer from the hottest band in the world shares the leftovers from his vegetarian dinner with his bass player? You must think I'm a moron."

"No. But I think you're completely prejudiced."

"What?" Summer faced Malcolm. She was seething with anger. "Did you just tell me I'm prejudiced?"

"Well, what would you call it?"

"Not being naïve?"

"But you are being naïve and prejudiced. You made a snap decision about me and someone else based on gossip you've heard because of my occupation. How would you like it if I assumed you were stupid because you're a model?"

"There are lots of models who are very smart." Summer spoke through clenched teeth.

"Yes. And there are musicians who don't treat women like rental cars."

"But you go through women—"

"Yes, maybe I do. But tell me something, Summer, why were you there tonight, huh? You told me you knew there was nothing permanent here."

He held up his hands, framing his torso. His abdominal muscles flexed as he spoke.

Malcolm continued in a softer voice. "You knew it was one night only. So why were you there? You must have wanted something just as much as I did. So why am I the only one to blame? Why weren't you using me just as much as I was using you?"

Summer stepped back, confused.

"And as far as Jimmy goes. Before you go running off to the gossip papers—he's a good guy. He's been married for twenty years. Twenty years on the road, and he's never cheated on his wife. Not once."

"Then why the—"

"Leftovers?" Malcolm smiled. "He's got high blood pressure. His wife put him on a vegetarian diet. He knew I'd ordered vegetarian and wanted to see if I had anything left. Room service screwed up his order. He's guilty of bad timing. Nothing else."

Summer felt herself deflate. "But why was he staring at me? At my breasts?"

"He's been married for twenty years." Malcolm grinned. "And in case you didn't know, you're a knockout."

Summer scoffed. "Hardly."

"So…" Malcolm clapped his hands together.

"What?" Summer felt like her entire world was upside down, and surprisingly, she didn't dislike the feeling.

"I'm ready for your apology."

"You have to be kidding."

Malcolm shook his head. "Nope."

Summer stepped back. "I—uh…" She tripped on her words. "Well then…"

Malcolm smirked at her, and Summer returned his smile with a glare.

She balled her robe in her fists, clenching and unclenching her hands. "I'm not sure…exactly…I mean, it's not every day…"

Malcolm swung his arms back and forth, obviously enjoying Summer's dilemma. "I'll tell you what." He stopped moving and spoke sincerely. "Since I can tell an apology will be tough for you, I'll let you off the hook. Have brunch with me tomorrow, and we'll call it even."

"Malcolm I—"

"You'd love to? Excellent."

"No. I mean, yes. Or, I don't know…" Summer could not remember a time she was so flustered. And looking at his strong, sexy body wasn't helping. "I couldn't…"

"Are you busy tomorrow at eleven?"

"No. But—"

"Eleven it is then."

Summer felt herself nodding without meaning to.

"Excellent." Malcolm turned toward the door and then back again. "I'll pick you up tomorrow morning at Jeanette's."

Summer nodded again.

"And by the way…" Malcolm smiled. "You really are more beautiful when you look like this." He started toward the door and turned back. "And you're even more beautiful when you're not yelling at me."

Malcolm clapped his hands again and didn't even try to hide the smirk on his face. He made his way out the door.

Summer stared after him as Jeanette waltzed into the living room.

"Summer, what just happened?"

"I think I'm going on a date with Malcolm Angel."

"Holy crap."

"Yup."

Both women stood perfectly still, staring at the closed door.

Chapter Seven

Summer checked the time. Ten forty-five.

She was wearing a yellow bra and her favorite faded jeans as she tore through Jeanette's enormous walk-in closet for the fourth time. She was adrift in a sea of high heeled shoes, white leather couches, and names on designer labels…some she couldn't even pronounce.

"I don't know why I'm doing this." Summer tossed the tag of a designer dress she had momentarily contemplated. It swung back and scratched her on the shoulder. She pouted, rubbing away the pain.

"Because you want to look sexy for your date with the hottest rock star in the world?"

"Oh, don't remind me." Summer slumped back against the opened door of Jeanette's closet. "And it's not a date." Through her sleepless night, Summer had rethought her position on brunch.

"Of course not. You're just dressing up and going to brunch. That never means a date." Jeanette giggled as she held up a turquoise gauze blouse, deciding how it would look on Summer.

"What I mean iiiissss…" Summer dragged each word out, as if lengthening her speech would somehow buy her more time. She tossed Jeanette's choice aside. "If he even bothers to show up…then this is some weird little game he's playing. He wants to make me suffer.

To humiliate me or something. Make me apologize for being prejudiced against his profession."

"Summer." Jeanette abandoned her clothing racks and moved closer to Summer. She placed a hand on Summer's arm. "Do you really think Malcolm Angel is going to waste his time playing some childish game?"

"I don't know what to think…or expect. In case you haven't noticed, I'm way out of my league here."

Jeanette squeezed Summer's hand. "You are certainly not out of your league. But you need to remember why you began this. It wasn't to get a boyfriend, Sum. You have to understand, you are a gorgeous woman who surprised Malcolm Angel. And I don't think that happens very often—if ever. So, he wants to see more. But remember, ultimately, he just wants to bed you. Which, as of last night, was all you wanted, too." Jeanette stared hard into Summer's eyes. "Is that true, Summer? Is that all you want?"

"Of course." Although Summer didn't believe in love, somehow, by the light of day, her plan to be *had* by Malcolm Angel seemed pretty cheesy.

"Okay." Jeanette stepped back, seeming satisfied with Summer's answer. "Then wear this." She handed Summer a white and yellow peasant blouse.

"Really?" Summer raised her eyebrows. "It's not very New York."

"That's why he'll love it." Jeanette nodded. "Besides, isn't it your lucky shirt?"

"Yes…"

"So maybe you'll get lucky in it then."

Jeanette smiled as Summer rolled her eyes, contemplating the blouse. Summer pulled the shirt over her head.

"Thanks, Jean."

"For what?" Jeanette was busy scrutinizing and fluffing Summer's hair. Summer batted her away.

"For all of it. And for leaving the hotel last night. You could have stayed. I would have been fine."

"I know." Jeanette shrugged. "But I was happy to have the company, too."

"He works a lot, huh?" Summer glanced at Jeanette out of the corner of her eye.

Summer had no opinion of Elijah, except he seemed to make Jeanette happy. He did keep very odd work hours, but what did Summer know about being the business manager of the hottest rock band in the world...? Maybe when he worked those late hours he was negotiating contracts with other parts of the world...places where our night was their day. The only other observation Summer had about Elijah was that he wasn't as attractive as the men Jeanette usually dated. He was early-sixties with a potbelly and a significantly receding hairline that he tried to comb-over. But surely, that would make him appreciate Jeanette, and her stunning beauty, all the more.

"Elijah? He works a lot."

"I guess." Jeanette shrugged away Summer's comment.

Okay, so obviously Jeanette didn't want to talk about this.

"Well, anyway, Jeanette. Thanks for always being there for me. Always."

Just then, Jeanette's doorman buzzed. Jeanette ran to the door, her excitement bubbling out of her.

"Yes?" Jeanette spoke into her intercom, still smiling at Summer. She motioned for Summer to put on some lip gloss.

Summer smeared on the lightest layer as Jeanette listened to her doorman's answer.

"Thank you." Jeanette turned to Summer. "It seems I was right. Security is waiting downstairs, and Malcolm Angel is heading up here. Thank heavens my Sunday doorman has no idea who Malcolm is." Jeanette giggled. "He's picking you up at the door, Summer. If that doesn't say date, I don't know what does."

Summer stared in disbelief as they both waited for Jeanette's doorbell to buzz.

****

Malcolm Angel had no idea what the hell he was doing. Why the hell had he made security wait downstairs? What if some deranged fan found him in the elevator? And why did he insist on meeting Summer at her door?

When he decided he wanted to take Summer to brunch, and she said yes, sort of…then one thing led to another until…well…one of his tour buses was parked outside her apartment building. Thankfully, years ago he had taken his name and likeness off his buses, so no one would know it was him. Now, the representation of him was nothing more than a big, shiny, empty, black bus.

It had started innocently enough. She made assumptions about him that…irked him for some reason, and he didn't know why. He knew what people said about him. He knew they thought he was scum, because he slept with a fair amount of women…okay, a lot of women…but it went with the territory. And although he didn't give a damn about what people thought of him, he was sure each and every woman he slept with understood they were there for one night only. But Summer…Summer was so self-righteous about it all, huffing and puffing while she fumed— totally off base—about being considered a "leftover." Malcolm chuckled, remembering Summer's cheeks turning flaming red, and the look of indignation on her face. All in all, it was pretty amusing. And annoying. And endearing…

But that wasn't the reason he was here. He snapped his fingers and clapped his fist against the flattened palm of his other hand. He wasn't here to set her straight. He was here because of the way she looked in that damned white robe. He smiled.

When the doors of the elevator slid shut, Malcolm caught his own reflection in the shiny metal and immediately looked down. He let his hands go limp, dangling by his sides. He had no interest in seeing himself. If he had his way, mirrors would be outlawed. He had to live with himself on the inside—why would he want to have to deal with the outside as well?

Malcolm shook his head, pushing his unsettling thoughts aside. What was it about this strange woman that was the catalyst of his uneasiness? Since he met her, only hours earlier, he had ridden a roller coaster of emotions, and he was ready to jump off the ride. Emotions were something Malcolm did not kowtow to.

Malcolm breathed deeply, squashing the ill-fitting sensation running up and down his veins. None of it mattered anyway—none of her appreciable qualities could mean anything—he didn't partake in relationships and after today, the only time he would ever run the risk of seeing her was when she was with Jeanette and Elijah. And that would only be a problem for the next few months, because Summer had assured him she was only here until Labor Day. And considering the plausibility of her modeling career, she would probably be gone even before then.

Malcolm frowned, exhaling a breath he didn't realize he had been holding. Although her absence was the answer to his predicament, he wasn't happy Summer was only temporary. He drew a sharp breath.

The elevator dinged, signifying his stop. As the floor leveled, Malcolm looked up and caught a glimpse of himself in the mirrored wall. Crap. He stared at the bags under his eyes and the lines on his face. Thirty-nine years old...damn. This is what hard living looks like. He shook his head and slunk off the elevator.

As he approached Jeanette's door, Malcolm could feel life throbbing inside. It was a sensation he never experienced walking up to his own apartment, not even with Winston waiting inside. The feeling he got as he approached Jeanette's door was enough to give Malcolm back his rock star swagger and to plaster a grin on his face. He stood outside Jeanette's door and leaned forward, straining to hear inside. Nothing. She was good. If she was nervous or giddy she wasn't going to let him know. He chuckled, imagining her expression when he took her outside and there was his tour bus...knowing her response would have to be either fight or flight but hell, he was ready for either. Deciding against the doorbell, Malcolm knocked on the door, liking the feeling of nearly touching Summer.

The door swung open and Malcolm felt a million little pin pricks stab him just so—like that time in Chinatown when he had endured a poorly executed acupuncture treatment. It wasn't particularly painful, but it wasn't entirely pleasurable, either. It was bearable. This was exactly what it felt like to stare at Summer in that light yellow and white top—so soft and full. For just a moment of time, Malcolm imagined falling against her breasts and weeping like he had never done. His eyes rose to hers, knowing the way he looked at her now may very well scare her off...forever. His chest heaved with his racing breath, and he was suddenly afraid she would be the arrow that would find the chink in his armor. But he couldn't let that happen. He breathed in deeply and stood up straighter and taller. He couldn't let any of it happen.

****

Summer slumped forward. For that split second when the door first opened, he looked genuinely happy to see her—but then, something changed. His face clouded over. Maybe seeing her in the light of day was a disappointment. She looked down at her outfit. Maybe Jeanette was wrong. Maybe her outfit was all wrong. She looked up and chewed her lip, staring at Malcolm. Maybe she was all wrong.

Summer hung back, confused. She wrapped one foot around the other leg, attacking her lip until it hurt. "Ow." She lifted her hand to her lip, assessing the damage.

"Wait." Malcolm was suddenly there, with a napkin he had grabbed off Jeanette's breakfast island. It was cloth, but he didn't seem to care if her blood stained it.

He placed the napkin to her lip and held it for her. He was so close now... Summer inhaled. He smelled like a medley of musk and sweat...he smelled, like darkness. She closed her eyes as he applied pressure,

71

but she was growing lightheaded. She needed to distance herself.

"Thanks." Summer stepped back and looked at Malcolm through heavy lashes, doing her best to deny the tingling sensation running up and down her body. The tingling came from the euphoria she was feeling, but why was she feeling euphoric when he held a napkin to her lip?

"Okay?" he asked.

Summer stared at his face, so worn and tired. He looked angry but hopelessly sad—that singularly unique look that until now, she had only ever seen on circus animals. Could the life of a celebrity be this trying? She nodded. "Yes, fine."

"Then let's get going."

And just like that the vulnerability faded, and he smiled his charming rock star smile. But it was there. And she had seen it. There was…something…hidden deep inside Malcolm Angel.

Summer slipped on her sandals and grabbed her bag, following him out the door.

****

"Uh, Malcolm…? What is this?" Summer used her thumb to point to the bus, as if she were hitching a ride.

"I told you I was taking you to brunch."

Malcolm walked ahead of her, but as he sauntered past, she saw he was fighting a smirk. He used the side of his fist to pound on the door of the tour bus, then stood to the side of the opened door.

Summer reached down and wiped her sweaty palms on her jeans. This was definitely a first. And he was definitely looking for a rise out of her. So there was no way he was going to get one. She raised her eyebrows and chewed the inside of her lip.

Summer waltzed by Malcolm and grabbed the handrail of the bus stairs. She tossed her long, loose hair as she spoke over her shoulder. "Oh, nice car, by the way." She smirked at him and turned back, hoisting herself up the stairs, feeling his eyes on her backside.

Just then a Golden Lab, nearly the size of Summer, jumped out and hugged her, his front paws resting on her waist.

"Oh!" Summer laughed happily, rubbing the dog's head. "Who is this?" She turned to Malcolm who was making his way onto the bus.

"Winston."

"Hello, Winston." Winston placed his paws on the ground but would not leave Summer's side. He pushed up against her legs, nearly knocking her over. Summer laughed, grabbing the pole at the stairs to balance.

"Sorry," Malcolm made his way around, trying to pull Winston off of Summer. "I guess I should have warned you."

"Warned me?" Summer kept petting the dog's head, playing with him. "Don't be silly. I love dogs."

"I can see that." Malcolm latched his hand to the back of his head. "I've never seen him react this way to anyone before." Malcolm suddenly went dark, and he walked to a window, gazing out.

"Oh, hey…" Summer followed Malcolm, with Winston at her heels. She giggled at Winston's whimpering, and then gave her full attention to Malcolm. "I'm sorry. Really. I'm just new and animals sometimes respond to someone new…that's all. I'm sure he'd be doing the same thing to you—and more—if I wasn't here."

Malcolm turned to face her. "That's what you think? I'm jealous?"

Summer shrugged. "Not jealous…"

Malcolm smiled in a way that touched Summer deep in her core. He reached out and placed his hand on her cheek. Summer inhaled and closed her eyes.

"I'm glad he likes you."

Malcolm dropped his hand, and Summer shivered in the void.

"He doesn't get to see many people, so I'm glad he's making a new friend."

Summer warmed with the idea of being one of the only people to meet Winston. Yes, it was irrational, but sometimes irrational felt good. "Well you should take him out more often. He's spectacular."

"Yeah," Malcolm nodded. "He is."

Malcolm offered Summer a seat on a forward facing couch. As soon as she sat, Winston put up his front paws and wiggled his backside, trying to jump onto Summer's lap.

Summer reached for him. "Is it okay?" Summer's eyes were big as she craned her neck to speak to Malcolm. "Do you mind if he sits up here with us?"

"Do I mind?" Malcolm chuckled. "I think I should be asking you that."

Summer smiled and hoisted Winston up onto the couch. Discreetly, she let her hand linger at Winston's leg and felt the stiffness in his hips. She wondered if Malcolm understood Winston was a very old dog, and what, ultimately, that meant. Before anyone could say another word, Winston plopped his head on Summer's lap and closed his eyes.

"I haven't seen him do that in…a very long time."

Malcolm sat next to Summer, with Winston between them.

"Jumping up?" Summer tried to question him casually.

"No." Malcolm shook his head. "Put his head on someone's lap."

Malcolm leaned forward, his legs relaxed, resting his elbows on his knees. Summer fought the urge to reach out and touch his back. He seemed like he could use a friend, and her desire to touch him was becoming intense. Instead, she busied her hands rubbing Winston's head, and discreetly studied Malcolm—his wide shoulders, his arm muscles straining to break free of his t-shirt... Uncomfortable in her current state of possibilities, Summer decided to fixate on something less distracting. Her eyes danced around the inside of the bus, glancing from the high-end kitchen to the areas separated by curtains.

"This is some bus. I never knew buses could be this nice."

"No?" He raised an eyebrow, looking at her.

"Nope." Summer scratched behind Winston's ears, lifting one and then the other.

"You've got an incredible gift with him."

"Thanks." Summer shrugged. "Anyway, it's only the three of us on the bus?"

"Plus the driver."

"Oh? You're not driving?" Summer smirked.

Malcolm grinned at her. "Not today. Anyway, that's why I brought Winston along. Just in case you thought I was up to something despicable."

Summer fidgeted in her seat, and Winston whimpered when she moved. "Listen," she lowered her voice not to bother Winston. "I really want to apologize about last night. I was wrong to think what I did and—"

"You were wrong. But I get it. I mean, with my reputation…I can only imagine what you must think."

Looking at Malcolm sitting next to his dog, there was no way he could possibly know what she was thinking. They took turns petting Winston's head.

"But I said terrible things. To you and Jimmy. Please send him my apologies. Or, I can write him a note and have Jeanette give it to Elijah—" Summer rubbed Winston's head so aggressively he whimpered. "Oh, sorry."

She pulled back, and Malcolm smiled.

"Summer, relax. Tell him yourself if you wanna."

"How am I going to do that?"

"I'll arrange it. Later in the week. Whaddaya say?"

What could she say? They were only minutes into their non-date, and already Malcolm had asked her on another. Or had he?

"Uh…Sure. Thanks. That would be really nice to have the opportunity to apologize—that is, if it's not too much hassle for you." Perspiration drenched the back of her neck, and her cheeks warmed. She fidgeted again.

Malcolm smiled. "Whaddaya say we head to brunch?"

"Sure." Summer busied her nervous hands by rubbing Winston's ears, much more carefully this time. "So uh, can you just do that?"

"What's that?" He turned to her, leveling his eyes on her.

Why did he always look at her like he was amused by her? Where was the joke?

"Can you just show up in some random place and have brunch? Won't you be stampeded or something?"

"Could happen." Malcolm shrugged. "But what are you gonna do? And besides, what makes you think any of this is random?" He raised an eyebrow.

The bus began to pull forward, and Summer lurched back in her seat. "Oh." She placed her hand on her chest to calm her racing heart. "Didn't know we were moving…"

Malcolm reached out and took Summer's hand in his. Summer turned to him, her eyes wide. She looked at their hands, his—so strong and capable—wrapped around hers. Her knees weakened, and she was thankful she was sitting down. It felt so…good…to have Malcolm's hand around hers. Too good, in fact. And as exciting as it was, she also felt safe—thanks to him. And safe was a feeling she couldn't ever remember feeling.

Summer looked away, and Winston readjusted, settling back to sleep. Summer breathed deeply, attempting to fight the sympathetic activity in her autonomic nervous system, oh the heck with it, the butterflies in her stomach—thrilled that Malcolm didn't move his hand from hers, not even when they picked up speed.

"Where are we going?" Summer finally found the nerve to look at Malcolm. When she did, she immediately shied from his relentless stare.

"It's a surprise." He spoke with his eyes locked on hers.

Summer nestled back, beaming. In the course of just a few hours with this man, he had unknowingly achieved nearly every to-do on her summer of irreverence checklist. She stole a peek at him out of the corner of her eye. Yes, Malcolm Angel was definitely a man. And she was definitely ready to be had by him.

****

When the bus pulled up beside the building on the Upper East Side, Malcolm silently prayed he could pull this off without fan interruption. He was certain Summer could handle it—the gawking, screaming, and crying—but the point was, he didn't want her to have to.

He had no idea why he was taking her to brunch. He could have easily asked her to rejoin him at his hotel—she might have said yes. But after last night's debacle, he didn't want to assume anything. Plus, he liked the fact that she stood up to him, so many other women simply said yes to whatever, because he was a famous singer. He never had the opportunity to be real. Didn't they understand that underneath the designer clothes he was a man? A man who wanted to be a man—and who wanted to treat her like a woman?

And besides, he liked prolonging the inevitable with Summer. It was the longest amount of foreplay he'd ever had…and it felt so good, he didn't want it to stop. Watching her breasts in that shirt was driving him wild. He had forgotten how much he loved full, voluptuous breasts. He also loved the curve of her jeans. He liked the feeling of anticipation. He hadn't felt that in… who knows how long. Everything was given to Malcolm immediately—from a table at a restaurant to sex—and this time he was spending with Summer was a very exciting, and welcomed, change.

"We're here Mr. Angel, sir."

Malcolm snapped out of his daydream and

reluctantly let go of Summer's hand. Winston poked his head up and yawned. He whimpered in anticipation. Malcolm understood entirely.

"Sorry, ol' boy. Not for you. And if you'll let your date go, she is expected upstairs with me."

Summer giggled, wiggling out from under Winston. Carefully, she laid his head on the seat.

"Good boy." Summer ruffled his fur, and Winston yipped in appreciation. She paused for a moment. "Um, Malcolm, how old is he?"

"Winston?"

She nodded.

"Not that old." He shrugged.

"Oh, okay." She looked back at Winston, petting him again.

"How old do you think?"

She stood up straight and tall and spoke with the most confidence Malcolm had ever seen from her.

"My guess? Seventeen or eighteen."

"That's a pretty accurate guess. He's eighteen."

Summer nodded, pursing her lips.

"How'd you know that?" Malcolm glanced at her sideways.

"Lucky guess." Summer adjusted her blouse and stuffed her hands into her front pockets.

Malcolm smiled at her—it was amazing that in the middle of Manhattan, she could look like such a clean, fresh, burst of nature. But still, he refused to be sidetracked.

"Really, how'd you know?"

Summer shrugged. "The gray hair I guess."

Malcolm ran his hand through his own hair. "Guess I should start taking him to my colorist."

Summer smiled, but Malcolm could see something was different in her eyes.

She recovered quickly, throwing her bag over her shoulder. "So, where are we heading?"

"You'll see…"

A knock on the bus door sent Malcolm into action. He walked to the back of the bus and grabbed a zip front sweatshirt. He pulled it on and threw the hood over his head. Summer was staring. "Don't worry. It's just 'til we get inside."

"Okay."

She still had that serious look on her face. The one that made Malcolm smile. He walked past her and stopped to tweak her nose before the door of the bus opened and his bodyguard walked in, carrying two sets of dark sunglasses. He handed one to each of them.

"It's just—"

"Until we get inside. I get it." Summer smiled and slipped on the glasses.

Her willingness to help and comply relaxed Malcolm. He never knew who he could ultimately trust. He looked over at Winston. Except, of course, for him.

****

Call it a vet's intuition, but Summer was greatly concerned about Winston. His age was obvious—sure his hair was graying, that really didn't mean much in the life of a dog, but he also appeared lethargic. No doubt he had the best medical care in the world, but even that couldn't stop the cloudiness in his eyes and the way he jumped up…with her needing to help scooch him upward. Summer sighed, fairly certain Winston was already, or would soon begin to, battle arthritis in his hips. What's more, she was sure he was showing signs of hip dysplasia; fairly common in larger breeds like Labs. And since Winston's condition was beginning later in life, it probably stemmed from the preexisting condition of osteoarthritis, which means even further deterioration of the joint was probable. Soon, Winston would need help to stand up and sit down, let alone to jump up onto a couch.

This was the part of her job she hated, having to relay bad news to pet owners, especially to someone like Malcolm who was so very attached to his pet. She sighed, hating more than her job right now—she hated herself for perpetuating the lie of being a model. For not coming clean and telling Malcolm he should have a support system in place, because the inevitable may be sooner rather than later. Watching Malcolm with Winston, all she wished was that she could tell the truth, but Jeanette warned her, over and over again, not to. To confess she was a vet would mean losing her one chance with Malcolm. And come on, he must have plenty of people to help him through whatever crisis he may face.

Gritting her teeth and deciding Malcolm surely had a team of veterinarians far more knowledgeable than herself on staff, she let the bad feelings pass. After all, she could be entirely wrong…although she knew in her gut she wasn't.

With her dark glasses on, Summer followed Malcolm and his bodyguard through a revolving door in an old, art deco hotel on the East Side.

She stifled a giggle when she walked in. "Do you ever go anywhere but hotels?"

Malcolm grinned at her, and taking her hand, he scooted her through the small hotel lobby, and silently led her into an old elevator, lined in ornate brass. Once inside, they both removed their glasses, and he pulled off his sweatshirt, exposing a fitted t-shirt and way too many muscles. The elevator was gorgeous, but tiny. She stood close to Malcolm, and heard the audible sound of her breath racing, as she wondered where, exactly, he was leading her?

The elevator fought its way up, toward the top floor. Strangely, Malcolm kept his eyes focused on the floor, as if he didn't want to see his own reflection. Summer shook her head. Why would that be? She could stare at him all day, every day.

As they climbed higher and higher, excitement had replaced the tension Summer was feeling earlier. When the elevator dinged, Malcolm stood to the side, holding his hand out to guide her way. She stepped through the elevator doorway and straight into... a construction zone. They were in the penthouse of this old hotel, and the building appeared to be falling down around them.

Summer shot a look at Malcolm, but there wasn't a single crack in his veneer. He remained stoic.

"C'mere..." Malcolm tossed his head. He held out his hand for Summer, and she slipped hers into his. "This way. Watch your step."

As they walked, making their way through a maze of rubble, cement blocks, and half erect walls, their hands stayed connected, momentarily bridging the endless gap between them. Finally, they stopped, and there, in front of her, in the middle of the chaos, sitting just before a floor to ceiling wall of windows, was a table, elegantly set for two.

Chapter Eight

A white tablecloth was draped over the small table, and two large, covered silver platters sat before two white upholstered chairs. The table and chairs rose above the rubble, sitting in complete juxtaposition to the rest of the room. Fresh daisies in a thin silver vase adorned the middle of the table. Water waited in crystal flutes, and a bottle of champagne was chilling beside the table.

Summer turned to Malcolm. "I…"

"Shh." He shook his head and squeezed her hand. "Just look." He nodded out the window.

Looking out at the city, Summer was certain she was trapped in a three-dimensional puzzle, with high rises both above and below her. Once, when she was a child, she played just such a game, where she rolled a silver ball along curved barriers inside a transparent globe. Looking down and then up, growing dizzy and then regaining her balance, Summer was now certain she was that ball. And looking at Malcolm, she knew he was the barrier.

"We're so high." Summer's voice was tiny and weak. She had never before felt so small.

Malcolm squeezed her hand and walked her to another window, this time, facing west. "I live over there." Malcolm raised his free hand, pointing to the opposite side of the city. "Jeanette's on the west side too, but way downtown."

Summer stood on her tiptoes to get a better view, and Malcolm smirked at her. He took her by the hand and pulled her into the space before him. He turned her shoulders to the left and leaned forward, letting his chin drop level to hers.

"That's Downtown." He pointed. "That's where you're staying."

Summer nodded, but as spectacular as the city was, he was even more so. She closed her eyes and leaned back into Malcolm's embrace. He turned her to face him, and they both grew very quiet. She could hear the sound of their breathing, both audible—although hers was much quicker. Malcolm didn't just stand in front of Summer, he commanded the space before her like he commanded a stage. She licked her lips, gazing up at him. He appeared younger now, not as haggard and tired. Although she could barely hold a cohesive thought, it made her happy to see him more relaxed. She was even happier to think she was the one who made him feel this way.

Malcolm leaned forward, framing her body with his arms, resting his hands on the metal window casings. He pushed her gently to the closest hard wall, readjusting so his hands could resume their possessive position behind her head. He leaned forward, and she nestled into the space created by his torso. She breathed in the feel of Malcolm, shrinking into herself, while his incredibly strong presence sheltered her. Her eyes traveled up his arms—hairy, scarred, and muscular—arms that could only belong to a man…and stopped when they made their way to the top of his t-shirt, where they feasted on one or two stray black hairs fighting their way free from his shirt. What were they thinking? If she had the opportunity to lie against Malcolm's chest, she would never leave. She shifted from foot to foot, fighting the growing ache in her body, caused entirely by his proximity. She arched her back slightly and sighed. Malcolm smiled.

Summer stared up into his eyes, black as a stormy night. He shifted to lean even closer to her.

She let out a small gasp as her chest heaved up and down. Although almost imperceptible, she sensed his eyes drop down, but she most definitely felt his fight to return them upward.

"I meant to tell you before, you look beautiful."

Summer's shoulders slumped with relief. "Thank you." Her cheeks burned, and she looked down. "I—I wasn't sure you liked my top, but it's my favorite."

Malcolm placed his finger under her chin and guided her eyes upward. "I think it's my favorite too." He smiled his wry rock star smile—the one that probably got him laid again and again...and, heck yes...again...

Summer bit down on her lip in the same spot she had drawn blood. "Ow." She put her fingers to her lip and rubbed.

Malcolm pulled her fingers away. He replaced them with his own. He rubbed his thumb against Summer's lip, gently.

"Does it hurt?"

Summer couldn't speak. She just shook her head no.

Carefully, Malcolm's forefinger parted her lips, and he dragged his finger into her warm, moistened mouth. "Your mouth...you...are so warm." He stepped closer to her. "And soft."

Summer's eyes darted up toward his. Perspiration dotted her forehead, and she felt her nipples harden. He tugged on her lip gently then let go, allowing his eyes to deliberately drop down to her shirt. He exhaled a deep guttural groan, and Summer felt an intense jolt of pleasurable pain flash through her body she couldn't—and didn't want to—explain with any logical medical reasoning. Her body moved toward his, and Malcolm lurched out, wrapping his arms around her waist, pulling her toward him with such force, she grunted. She pressed against him, and he held her tightly, his black eyes warming.

"I don't even know your last name..." he whispered.

Summer exhaled, frustrated, feeling the moistness in her jeans, knowing there was no way to maintain their intensity once she spoke.

"Okay."

He held her at arms' length. "Okay? Your last name is 'Okay'?"

She rolled her eyes. "No, it's okay you don't know."

His eyes clouded over, and he let his hands slide down her arms until they were no longer touching. A searing pain socked Summer in her gut. She'd have to tell him, or risk hurting him. She stood up straight, and shimmied around a bit, trying to alleviate the contact from the seam of her jeans. Why did he stop?

"Okay, okay...I'll tell you. But please try to keep your reaction under control."

Malcolm raised his eyebrows. "I'll make no such promise."

Summer blushed. "You know what I mean..." Her voice was a mere whisper.

"Okay, fine. I will do my best. But why are you anticipating a reaction? What could your name possibly be?" Malcolm twisted his mouth as he spoke. He squinted as he offered possible options. "Summer Smith? Summer Saunders...Summer Day?" His eyes sparkled. "That's it, isn't it? Summer Day?"

"Wynters."

"Excuse me?" The look of entertainment came back to Malcolm's face.

Summer rolled her eyes again and crossed her arms. "You heard me."

She turned to walk away, but Malcolm grabbed her hand and held her fast.

"Oh, no. No way. You can't drop that and then just walk off. Did you just say, 'Winters'?"

"Yes."

"As in, Summer Winters...?"

"Yes. But it's not spelled like you're thinking. It's W-Y-N-T-E-R-S."

"I don't think that's any better." Malcolm laughed.

Summer smiled and pouted, playfully storming away. She made her way around the construction zone and back to the table with Malcolm at her heels. "That is the reason I didn't want to tell you." Her voice was high, enjoying the banter.

"How did you go through life with that name...?" Malcolm's eyes flashed with happiness. "I mean, if I wrote it, people would crucify me. What were your parents thinking?"

Summer froze.

"I mean, do they love you at all?" Malcolm

chuckled.

Summer's feet refused to move, and her arms lay limp at her side.

"Summer?" Malcolm's smile faded. "Sum?"

The sound of her nickname spoken by Malcolm did her in. She desperately fought the mounting tears.

Malcolm stared at her. "It's not your name you're upset about, is it?"

Summer clenched her jaw and shook her head.

"I'm sorry." His voice was low and modulated.

She nodded, looking at Malcolm, and wanting, for the first time ever, to have someone make it all okay. To have him make it all okay.

Malcolm grew quiet. They stood there for whole minutes. "I'm sorry if I touched on a sore subject. Really."

Summer stared at him—this man who had everything except the answer she needed. How could he be so closed off? How could he care so little about the pain of another living creature?

He stepped forward then, as if reading her mind, took her hand gently, and leaned over, speaking quietly into her ear. "It's not that I don't care." Those few words found a place deep in Summer's soul.

Malcolm stood tall, and Summer's eyes followed him. He reached out and stroked her cheek. "But I've got nothing more to give than today."

Chapter Nine

Summer had a choice. She could leave or stay. But why would she leave? She didn't believe in love, and she knew he wasn't here for the long haul. She wasn't expecting him to become her boyfriend, she was simply momentarily caught up in…him. In his intensity and power. He had the ability to fulfill her every immediate desire, and she went into this with eyes opened. She knew she had only one night with Malcolm Angel, it's just that their one night was lasting the entire weekend.

Summer swallowed hard and smiled. "So, what's this meal you have planned? I'm famished."

Malcolm smiled at her then, his eyes eternally grateful.

"Right this way…" He held up his hand and together, they made their way to the small table waiting for them.

"This is incredibly beautiful." Summer scooted her chair forward as Malcolm slid the chair in for her. She nearly swooned at his gentlemanly behavior. Wasn't it enough that he was incredibly bad-boy hot? Did he have to draw her in so completely? He sat across from her, placing his elbows on the table and resting his chin on his hands. The ring he wore on his right hand middle finger, a flat silver barrel wrapped around his finger, caught her eye. He just sat, waiting. He looked like the male blackbuck, leading an elaborate courtship with horns held back—and Summer was more than willing to be part of his mating ritual, fully understanding he would soon run off with the next unsuspecting female antelope that caught his fancy. She giggled at the thought of Malcolm with long spiraled horns, thinking it was a fairly accurate zoomorphic description for him.

"What are you giggling about?"

Summer nearly forgot he could hear her giggle. She shook her head. "I'm just a little overwhelmed. This is…" She shook her head.

With that, Malcolm stood and whisked the top off her brunch. Summer stared at her plate.

"We have warm eggplant and olive pâté with pita chips to start, cauliflower with papaya chutney, and a Thai coconut lemongrass curry with jasmine rice. Hope you like it." His eyes told her he really meant it.

"Like it? Malcolm it's...it's…thank you." She had to look away from him, his presence was almost too much. She risked another glance at him, and her heart rate responded accordingly. "But how did you get all of this ready so quickly?"

He smirked and raised his eyebrows. "Really?"

"Oh," Summer covered her mouth with her hand. "I forgot for a moment." She looked up at him. "It must be amazing to be you."

Darkness flashed across his eyes. "Amazing is not the word I would use."

Summer shrugged and picked up her fork. She twirled it. "Well, it's amazing to be with you, that's for sure."

He smiled.

****

"Champagne?" Malcolm held up a bottle to show

her, but Summer waved it away.

"No, thank you." She shook her head. "After last night I think I'm done with champagne for awhile."

"You had two glasses."

She leaned forward, gripping the table. "And apparently that was two more than I should have had."

"Nah." Malcolm winked at her.

Summer's eyebrows knitted together in that adorable way they do when she's serious. He knew what was coming.

"Let me just say, again…" she gripped the table tighter. "I am truly sorry for misjudging you. I—I was wrong."

"Summer…" he leaned across and took her hand.

Her eyes dashed up to his.

"Just forget it. Really. It was, rather amusing."

He smirked at her, and she beamed at him.

Warning signals flashed through his head. What the hell was he doing? He released her hand and took a bite of his food. Damn it, everything tasted better than usual. And he knew why. It was thanks to Summer sitting across from him, and frankly, that wasn't okay.

Although he allowed himself the pleasure of female company—frankly, in his profession he would be dead without the stress release sex offered—he never allowed himself attachment. It was okay for his body to feel good…but his soul…that was something else entirely.

Malcolm would remain a tortured artist until the day he died, and no amount of casual conversation with a gorgeous, bright, blonde woman, who happened to be incredibly good with his dog, would change that. He invited her to brunch only to set the record straight. He chose the deserted location only out of necessity. He ordered an elaborately set table and brunch only because he could. It had nothing to do with pleasing her. Nothing at all.

Malcolm felt the scowl on his face and saw the return of worry etched in her forehead. He wished he could tell her his melancholy had nothing to do with her, but the truth was, it had everything to do with her.

"So what is your deal, Summer Wynters?" Malcolm leaned back, fiddling with his butter knife, studying Summer.

"What do you mean?"

"I mean…" He sat forward now and felt the reaction in her body even across the table. God she was beautiful. And ripe. And incredibly warm and sexy. He fought to keep his hands to himself—how desperately he wanted to slide them inside her shirt, letting them find their way to her round, soft breasts. He breathed deeply, envisioning her nipples stiff between his strong, experienced fingers, his mouth plastered to hers—her moan filling his very core. He shook his head. "What are you doing here?"

"You asked me." Summer raised her water glass, toasting.

"Touché. But you know what I mean. Why is Summer Wynters out with Malcolm Angel?"

Summer placed her water glass down and leveled her eyes on Malcolm. "Malcolm. I don't know any woman in the world who would not want to be sitting here right now."

He nodded, while disappointment burned a gaping hole in his stomach. What did he think she was going to say? Why was any woman ever with him except for the fact that he was Malcolm Angel? Did he think she had special powers in those amazing green eyes, allowing her to see through the years-old veneer he plastered on his soul? Could he really expect someone to like him for being more than Malcolm Angel, when he'd never allow her to know who that was? And if she did know the real him...No. Not today. Malcolm looked away.

"I mean, can you blame me?"

Malcolm turned back to face her, forcing a tiny smile.

"He is just spectacular."

Malcolm sat forward, studying her out of the corner of his eye. He squinted. "Excuse me?"

"Winston. He is just spectacular. Why else would I be out to brunch with you?" She took a bite of her breakfast, smiling victoriously.

The laugh started in Malcolm's gut and made its way up and out, surprising him with its ferocity. Summer laughed too, and Malcolm saw tiny crinkles form around her eyes when she did. Somehow, they made her even more beautiful. He stared at her face, barely made up, with the softest touch of blush and mascara. She was more than beautiful. She was stunning. And sharp.

"Thing is," Malcolm leaned forward, resting his arms on the table. "You said yes before you met Winston."

"Touché." She stopped laughing and looked down at the table.

"So, out with it. What are you up to?"

She looked up at him with eyes that were full of answers, although he knew she'd never share them.

"I have a summer. One summer. For me. And I

wanted to do things I've never done before. I want," her words were thick, but she pushed on, "I want to get as far away from me as possible."

"Why would you wanna do that? You seem pretty great to me." His head snapped backward, the vulnerability in his voice surprising him.

She swallowed hard and nodded slightly. "Something tells me, Malcolm, you of all people understand needing to escape."

Malcolm exhaled audibly.

****

Summer loved that they sat close to each other, side by side on the couch of the tour bus. Malcolm leaned down to help Winston up onto their laps, and the medal he wore around his neck hung forward. Summer reached out and grasped it. Malcolm froze, his eyes fixed on the ground before him.

"Saint Francis of Assisi… huh." Summer smiled. "I've seen that silver chain around your neck in pretty much every picture I've ever seen of you. I never knew there was a medallion attached to it. I never would have guessed what was on it."

St. Francis of Assisi—the patron saint of animals. Darn it. This guy was really going to be in for some significant pain. Summer petted Winston's head, and he wheezed in response. And unfortunately, this pain was going to come sooner rather than later.

Malcolm sat back, stiffly. He crossed his legs, resting his ankle on his opposite knee. He leaned forward. Every ounce of him looked uncomfortable. Something was wrong.

"Oh, I—uh, I'm sorry. I didn't realize I shouldn't have seen that."

"No, no…" Malcolm looked away. "It's fine."

Summer turned to Malcolm, sighing. "Obviously, judging from your body language, it's not fine."

Malcolm turned to her. "It's…just…private. I take it off whenever I know my shirt will be off."

Summer smirked at him. "Didn't think your shirt was coming off around me, hey?" She nudged him in the shoulder.

He raised his eyebrows. "Given the opportunity, I'd snap that necklace off damn quick."

Summer giggled, then composed herself. She bit the inside of her cheek. "Malcolm. I want you to know something. I—I liked spending time with you today. But really, it wasn't about being with Malcolm Angel."

He uncrossed his legs and leaned forward. Summer rolled her shoulders, feeling the disconnect between she and Malcolm.

"All I'm trying to say is, your secret is safe with me. Really. You have a right to your privacy, and I respect that. Please don't worry I would do something tacky like sell the scoop to some trash magazine. Truth be told, I've never read a single one of them, and I wouldn't harm another living soul for financial gain or fifteen minutes of fame. It's just not me."

He tilted his head upward, and for a moment, relief tinged the permanently etched worry on his face. She knew then that he believed her.

They sat elbow to elbow, staring straight ahead. Malcolm reached out and took Summer's hand, squeezing so tightly, she shed a tear…not from physical pain, but because of the pain she felt for him. She sat, her back plastered to the seat, her free hand wiping her tear, desperately fighting the urge to take him into her arms. Winston looked up at her, his eyes cloudy and mournful…and Summer understood then, her summer of irreverence had just become her summer of empathy.

Chapter Ten

"Friends?" Jeanette stormed across her living room and stood, blocking Summer's way. "I invested an entire weekend of my life to your cause...to your dire need to be *had*, and you're telling me you're just friends?"

"Well—"

"No." Jeanette put up her hand, cutting Summer off. She paced to her couch and back to Summer. She opened her mouth as if she was about to speak, then returned to the couch again.

Summer had yet to enter the apartment. She hung by the door, clutching her tote. She slipped off her sandals and rubbed a sore foot.

Jeanette approached again. "You're telling me you went to a deserted hotel...with Malcolm Angel...and nothing happened?"

"We—"

"And you were with him—alone—on one of his tour buses and still nothing happened?"

"It was a—"

"There are beds on those buses you know."

"How do you—"

"Never mind how I know, I just do."

Jeanette slumped down onto the couch as Summer giggled. Summer walked to Jeanette, approaching cautiously.

"Can I speak now?"

"Please." Jeanette pulled a pillow onto her lap and pouted. "It's just…he might just be the sexiest man alive. How could you not?"

"He didn't ask." Summer plopped down next to Jeanette and pulled another throw pillow onto her lap.

"What?" Jeanette turned to Summer, her eyes wide. She tucked her hair behind her ears.

"I guess he's not into me."

"Wait, wait, wait." Jeanette sat forward, adjusting herself. "Did he say that?"

"No…"

"Did he tell you, you looked nice?"

"He said my shirt was his favorite. And I was beautiful." Summer bit her lip, trying to remain stoic, but her smile quickly took over.

"Anything else?"

Summer shrugged.

"Sum?"

"He held my hand."

"He what?"

Jeanette was up out of her seat so quickly, Summer wondered if she shouldn't have said anything.

"Shh…" Summer stood, hushing Jeanette. "It's not a big deal."

"Oh, that is such a big friggin' deal." Jeanette bounced to her refrigerator and grabbed two cans of diet soda. She handed one to Summer.

"No, thanks. You know that stuff is terrible for you."

"I just have to right now. Hold on. Malcolm Angel didn't sleep with you, but he held your hand?"

"Yes. And now I'm here. He was exceptionally

nice about the whole thing, and it was incredibly…exciting…all of it. But it's over now." Summer fought the rising panic she felt in her chest. Anxiety attacks can be natural occurrences when someone is placed in foreign situations, like luxury brunches in decrepit buildings with sexy rock stars. Unfortunately, this panic attack was not founded in stress, it stemmed from the idea of never seeing Malcolm again. She sighed. At least she had brunch with him. That was more than most.

"Sum," Jeanette sat next to Summer and stroked her hair. "I knew this would happen."

"What?" Summer didn't try to fight the tears in her eyes. "You knew he wouldn't want me?"

Jeanette's lips curled into a smile. "Oh, I'm sure he wants you. That's not up for debate. I just don't understand why he's delaying…" Jeanette looked off and shook her head. She shimmed around on the couch and took Summer's hand. "Anyway. I knew you would fall for him. Even you couldn't be immune to his charms."

"I am certainly not immune, but I didn't 'fall for him'." Summer took her hand back, making air quotes. "And I am not heartbroken, because there is no such thing as a broken heart. What bothers me is that…" Summer turned away.

"What?"

Summer turned back to Jeanette. She had known Jeanette almost her entire life, and they were as close as two friends could be. But Summer knew what was happening…or correction, what had happened with Malcolm was something she couldn't explain to anyone. And frankly, no one else deserved to know.

"Romantic love doesn't exist, Jeanette. It's made up by the card companies who want us to spend more money on holidays." Summer squeezed her friend's hand. "But friendship does exist. And sexual attraction certainly exists, it's how our species survives."

Summer wanted to explain more to Jeanette, to tell her about Winston, and how she was worried, but the lump in her throat and the agitation in her stomach told her to remain mum. She pursed her lips.

"So let me get this straight…" Jeanette held up her fingers, as if she were going to start checking off inconsistencies in Summer's logic.

"Brrinnnggg!"

Summer jumped. Saved by the ring. Mumbling something about being interrupted at the best part, Jeanette got up and made her way to the breakfast bar to retrieve her phone.

"Hello?" She leaned against the counter as she spoke.

Summer stared at Jeanette's back, deciding what she could honestly share with her friend. Short of the medal, it wasn't as if anything all that private happened. How do you explain a connection, anyway? That is, if there really was a connection.

Jeanette stood up tall and frantically waved Summer over. Summer stood, as her heart sped up, palpitating. She bolted to Jeanette's side, terrified something horrific had just happened…experiencing a wretched bout of déjà vu.

"What?" Summer stood too close to Jeanette. A drop of fear-induced sweat trickled down her spine, and she wrung her cold hands. "Jeanette? What? Your parents okay?"

"She's right here." Jeanette smirked at Summer, holding the phone out to her. "It's Malcolm. Said he never got your cell number, so he called mine." Jeanette raised her eyebrows, pushing the phone at Summer.

Summer backed away, shaking her head. Instead of relaxing her already agitated state, his call made her all the more frantic. "No," she whispered. "No, no, no..." Relief and terror began their war in Summer's gut, and she placed her hand on her tummy.

"Hold on, Mal..." Jeanette covered the phone as she spoke. "I will tell the man you are in the bathroom if you don't answer."

"You wouldn't." Summer stepped forward.

"I'll tell him the brunch he fed you made you sick."

Summer glared at Jeanette. Yup. Jeanette's insanely competitive spirit would make her capable of just such a thing.

"Fine." Summer snatched the phone away from Jeanette.

Jeanette sauntered to the couch.

"He—hello?" Summer's voice cracked, and she moved her mouth away from the receiver to clear her throat. "Oh, hi." She shook her head, knowing her casual tone wasn't fooling anyone.

"I had to call." Malcolm's voice was clear and energetic. Very different from how he sounded on the bus.

"Okay. I—I'm glad you did." Summer turned her back to Jeanette, like a teenager desperate for privacy in a house full of family.

"I wanted to call anyway, but Winston here insisted I do it now. Before you made other plans."

"Other plans?" Summer gripped the phone tightly

and inadvertently pushed a button. A loud "beep!" rang through her ears, and she pulled the phone away from her head. She returned it immediately.

"Malcolm?"

"Here."

"Sorry. I…I'm not used to Jeanette's phone." Or casual conversations with rock stars.

"No problem. So Winston and I were wondering if you'd wanna go to the dog park with us. Tomorrow. If you're not busy."

Summer blinked repeatedly and scoffed. "I'm not busy, Malcolm, and I would very much like to. What time?"

"I figure you've got go-sees in the morning, and I've gotta go to the studio, so how 'bout afternoon? Four? We can grab dinner after."

Summer cringed at the word, "go-see." The stabbing pain in her head warned her she had to tell Malcolm the truth. She was not, and never would be, a model. But she knew she couldn't. He couldn't be seen with a woman who wasn't a model, and there was no way he'd stick around if he found out she was fibbing. She swallowed hard. "Sounds perfect. I think I heard of a building they are demolishing in Hell's Kitchen tomorrow. I expect we'll be dining there?"

"Ha," Malcolm laughed. "You're something, kid. I'll pick you up tomorrow at four. See ya."

"Bye."

Summer hung up the phone but stood staring at the kitchen wall. "I know what you're doing, Jean."

"You do not."

Summer turned around and smirked as Jeanette danced her way across the apartment and over to

Summer. She grabbed Summer and spun her around and around.

"Sum…" Jeanette's cheeks were flushed, and she was radiant. "You are Malcolm Angel's girlfriend."

Summer broke away from Jeanette, scoffing. "Please."

"Well, what would you call it? You…you're dating Malcolm Angel."

"I'm spending some time with a friend. That's all."

"Really?" Jeanette grinned. "That's all, huh?"

"Yes." Summer shrugged her shoulder. "Just a really, really, incredibly sexy friend…"

****

Malcolm strolled next to Summer, with Winston walking ahead of them. Malcolm's bodyguard hung a few feet behind them. It was warm today, too hot for the hoodie and dark glasses, but what choice did he have? He stole a glance at Summer who was also wearing dark glasses. She looked incredibly sexy in her tan shorts and white t-shirt. She couldn't possibly know what her long toned legs were doing to him. And that t-shirt—the way it pulled ever so slightly across her breasts—not overtly, just perfectly. She was gorgeous.

He would love to see her in one of his band's t-shirts. Just the t-shirt and panties… Malcolm's eyes dropped down to her backside, and he strained to see what sort of panties she was wearing. A thong? Nah, he shook his head. Pink silk? Maybe. White cotton? There was a real possibility there. Especially if they were decorated with just the slightest bit of lace… Malcolm sidestepped for a moment, trying to fight his growing attraction to her. Running pants were definitely not a good choice when he was spending time with Summer.

And why, exactly, was he spending time with Summer? What was he doing? Damn. Malcolm stepped aside again, trying to remain inconspicuous. Deciding what panties Summer Wynters wore was maybe his most favorite game—ever. But it was also an uncomfortable one. Malcolm gritted his teeth and forced his thoughts onto jellybeans. He hated jellybeans. Maybe they would help.

She turned to him and smirked.

Not helping. Nothing was helping. Malcolm stuffed his hand into his pocket. "What?"

"We look like two people who just had their eyes tested for glaucoma." She giggled.

"Ha." He snickered. "Good thing Winston's leading the way."

"Yeah." Summer bolted ahead a few steps and petted Winston. He barked, happily. She turned back to face Malcolm, walking backwards as she spoke.

Malcolm fought to keep his eyes on hers, but with the dark glasses…

"I never knew this place existed."

Summer's voice was soft and filled with energy. It warmed his already overheated core, promising him everything would be okay—even when he knew that wasn't possible.

"Yeah—" he cleared his throat. "It's pretty secluded. With a great view of the East River." There was a view he was enjoying even more, however.

"Do you wear that all summer?" She stopped and placed her hands on her hips.

"What's that?"

"The sweatshirt. Doesn't it make you hot?" She joined him now, falling into time alongside him.

"Better than the alternative." He shrugged.

"Which is?"

As she spoke, he watched the softness and swell of her chest rising and falling.

"Being clawed to death, probably."

Summer stopped short and turned to him. Malcolm stopped with her.

"Is that true?"

She whispered the words, leaning toward him. He caught a whiff of her—she smelled clean and pure, like laundry fresh off a clothesline. Her body trembled slightly, and he fought his desire to take her hand to reassure her. Sometimes being a celebrity really sucked—like right now, when all he wanted was to hold the hand of a girl he liked, in a dog park, with his dog. But protocol said no way. Because if someone figured it out and snapped their picture, that would be the end of their privacy.

Malcolm saw real concern in her tense body. "Nah." He waved the thought away. "Fans can just get a little crazy sometimes, that's all."

"I can't even imagine." Summer shook her head. They ambled forward and the way she walked, casual and relaxed, she looked young and sweet.

"Would you wanna?" He came to a quick halt, praying she wouldn't read into his question.

"Me? Fame? No way. I prefer to remain anonymous. Crowds are not my thing."

"Strange." Malcolm tilted his head, trying to offer her an out. He really didn't care she wasn't a model. It meant nothing to him. Actually, it was a refreshing change to spend time with someone who wasn't constantly taking selfies and checking her number of followers on Instagram.

"Why's that?"

"Usually women who are models are happy with as much publicity as they can get."

"Oh." Summer turned her eyes to the ground and sighed. She kicked a stone away, swallowing hard.

Why wouldn't she just tell him? His hands were tied. He couldn't ask—she would take it as an insult, for sure. And the last thing he wanted to do was to insult her.

She pushed her hair behind her ear, and a tiny pearl balanced delicately on her earlobe. Synthetic for sure. Malcolm breathed deeply, fighting his possessive instinct, wanting desperately to pull her into the nearest jewelry store to replace those fake orbs with dazzling, large, real pearls. Wanting to claim her ears…and the rest of her…as his. But he couldn't.

She smiled at him awkwardly, biting the corner of her lip. He knew soon enough she would clamp down on her nearly healed lip and possibly draw blood again. How strange he had already learned her tells. He glanced at her out of the corner of his eye and wondered if she knew his.

She knitted her eyebrows together and focused hard on the ground before them. He really didn't want her to hurt herself. Oh, the hell with it. He reached out and took her hand, intertwining his fingers with hers. He hoped she would understand he knew, and it was okay.

She stopped short and turned to him.

"Malcolm, I…" She was struggling, chewing her lip and sighing.

Obviously, she wasn't ready to tell him. He needed

to let her off the hook.

"Hey. No more shop talk. K?"

She smiled.

"Whaddaya say we let Winston off his leash? He's dying to show you what he's got."

Malcolm's brain fought his hand, but finally, he let go so she could attend to Winston. She nodded eagerly, squatting down to pet Winston, and Winston reciprocated by licking her face.

Summer stood, giggling, as Winston took off after a pigeon. He was happy, running like a dog half his age. Maybe all those supplements Malcolm fed Winston were helping. Especially the ones for his joints.

Summer grabbed a tennis ball out of her bag and darted from Malcolm's side. It was odd, but he felt the void the moment she left... She threw the ball for Winston. He chased it down and went running back to her. Over and over she would pet his head and kiss him. Over and over Winston would come running back to her. Malcolm understood completely.

Malcolm gazed at Summer. She looked so young and joyful all he wanted was to preserve this moment. His chin dropped low as he stared at her. He wanted to be with her. Really be with her. The muscles in his shoulders tensed and spread wider, and he stood up, taller. He felt primal...possessive. He fought to stay still—his hands clenched and unclenched, and perspiration dripped down his back. He felt like a man.

Summer suddenly stopped playing with Winston. Still holding the ball, she looked over at Malcolm, put up her hand, and gave an intimate wave. She smiled.

Malcolm smiled back.

He hated that he was going to destroy her.

Chapter Eleven

Two days together passed into two weeks. During that time, Summer spent every day with Malcolm Angel. Somewhere along the way he had told her he would like to help her experience all those things she had never before experienced, and he made good on his promise. Together they had dined in some of the most private and exclusive restaurants in Manhattan and surrounding boroughs. On those trips to and from the restaurants, they sat together in the back of his limo, holding hands, heat radiating off of them. They also took taxis to eat in some of the most secluded divey hangouts in the East Village, where no one gave a darn about Malcolm Angel, and he seemed pretty okay with that.

One time, he took her to his studio where she heard him record his newest song. He was magic to watch—strong, vibrant, incredibly sexy. She knew he was an immensely talented musician, but as she watched him attack his sheet music with a pencil and eraser, she learned what a perfectionist he was. He brought her to listen in on rehearsal. She sat for hours, mesmerized, as from the intangible he strung together lyrics and harmonies, pulling from this, adding to that, until he had given it shape—until he had given it life. She sat on the couch opposite his recording room, watching. As he sang, tears sprang into her eyes…tears she never bothered to wipe away. When he finished, he came directly to her and wiped them for her.

They also spent time with Winston daily, which gave her the opportunity to monitor any changes in Winston's behavior that might warrant immediate action. But so far, they were lucky.

With Memorial Day behind her, Summer could relax more. Every day that Malcolm asked her out for the next she was surprised, but she loved being with him. Although he had yet to kiss her, they held hands constantly, like high school sweethearts.

The only thing really bothering Summer was that Dr. Brad would call her from time to time. And today…well, that Malcolm Angel hadn't.

"Ugh." Summer's blasted phone rang again, and gosh darn it, it was Dr. Brad. Again.

"Just tell him you're dating Malcolm Angel," Jeanette quipped not looking up from her magazine. "Hey…do you like this picture of me?" She held up a multipage editorial ad in the magazine.

Summer buried her phone in Jeanette's couch, trying to suffocate the obnoxious ringtone.

"You could just block his calls."

"I'm not dating Malcolm. We're just friends." Summer sighed and held out her hand. "Let me see the pictures." She spoke loudly to block the sound of the phone. She took the magazine, looking at four pages of Jeanette on a beach, wearing nothing but perfume. "Jeanette, they're gorgeous. Why would you even ask? You're in tons of magazines and ads and you never ask." The ringing stopped, and Summer forced her shoulders away from her ears, looking at her friend. "Why are you asking, really?"

"I've never been twenty-nine before." Jeanette crossed and uncrossed her legs, her slip skirt riding high on her skinny legs.

"You're not twenty-nine." Summer pushed the magazine back to Jeanette and picked up her cell.

"I will be. In a couple of weeks."

"Is that what this is about?"

"Why aren't you blocking Dr. Brad's calls?"

"Because I'm a grown-up."

Jeanette sighed. "A grown-up who gets to stay twenty-eight for another six months."

Summer glanced at her texts, ignoring Jeanette. "Brad is an immensely talented doctor whom I will be working with this fall. He will be my boss—whether I like it or not. And to block him would be immature, unnecessary, and detrimental. He'll take the hint. It won't take him long to find a new girlfriend." Summer thumbed through the magazine, turning pages without seeing pictures.

"Unless he doesn't want to."

"He has to." Summer tossed the magazine aside and checked her phone again. "Why are you so worried about your birthday? I mean, really?"

"Is there a reason you keep checking your phone?"

"I'm not." Summer passed the phone to her other hand.

"Okayyyy…"

"So what's the deal with your birthday?" Summer took a deep breath, focusing on Jeanette.

Jeanette picked up the magazine and flipped to the ad she had shown Summer. "See the eye in this close up?"

"Yeah?"

"Look closely."

Summer squinted to get a better look. "Beautiful. It's—"

"Not mine." Jeanette plopped the magazine down.

"What?" Summer picked it up, staring again.

"It's not mine. Eyes don't photograph well after twenty-five, so..."

"That's a thing?" Summer raised her eyebrows. "Good grief." Summer's phone vibrated, and she nearly dropped it looking at the text. Her shoulders slumped, and she fought back tears when she read the reminder text from her dentist. For an appointment that was over two months away. Darn it. Sometimes she really hated technology. "It uh," she fought hard to remain calm. "It's crazy. Why would you stop photographing eyes over—"

"He hasn't called you yet today?"

Summer shook her head, terrified if she spoke, she would begin sobbing and never stop.

"That's why you're not dressed?"

Summer nodded.

"Oh, Sum." Jeanette moved closer to her on the couch. "I'm sorry. I feel like a jerk for sitting here like this."

"No, no. You look gorgeous. And Elijah is your boyfriend. You should be going to this party. The chances of Malcolm asking me as his date...we both knew that was nearly impossible. I'm sure he'll bring that girl from your agency...what was her name? The one who went out with him for publicity." Summer's throat ached, and the tears mounded in her eyes. Although she didn't believe in romantic love or heartbreak, she sure believed in physical pain stemming from severe disappointment. She glanced at the dress Jeanette had given her, hanging on the door of Jeanette's closet. Summer clutched her stomach, her dinner threatening to come back up.

"Sometimes the choice isn't his, Sum. Sometimes his management picks his date."

"Well if that's the case, they're certainly not going to pick some five foot six country girl with big hair and giant boobs." Summer sank back into the couch, pulling the pillow onto her lap.

"You don't have big hair…" Jeanette sat beside her. "And you're beautiful. And being Connecticut born and raised hardly makes you a 'country girl,' thank you very much. And yeah, okay, you've got big boobs, but I'll bet he likes them."

"Who knows?" Summer turned to Jeanette. "I sure as heck don't. It's not like he ever tries to see them."

"Summer…" Jeanette's voice was soft. "There could be a million reasons he hasn't called. He's incredibly busy. He's Malcolm Angel."

"I know." Summer's words were broken and weak. "Sometimes….sometimes I just wish he wasn't."

Jeanette reached out and wrapped her arm around Summer's shoulders. "Want to come with me?"

Summer shook her head no. "Thanks. No. That's the last thing I want to do. It'll look like I'm stalking him."

Jeanette nodded. "Want me to stay home, and we can order in?"

Summer smiled at Jeanette, knowing Jeanette would do just that. "No. Thank you, though. I'm going to stay here and do some reading. I have some medical journals to catch up on. Hanging out with a rock star all summer has kept me from my real world."

"Okay." Jeanette stood, smoothing her little black dress and running her hand down her long, silky ponytail. "And don't worry. I will give you a full report on who she was and what she looked like."

Summer scoffed. "No thanks. I'll pass. All I want to do right now is escape back home to my clinic and get lost among the animals. I can trust them."

"You can trust the right men, too." Jeanette put her hand on Summer's and squeezed.

Summer shivered from the cold. "You're freezing, Jean. You should eat more."

"Please, I'm almost twenty-nine. If I started eating…" She laughed, not finishing her thought.

Summer shook her head, exhausted from all the worry that fell on her today.

"Okay." Jeanette checked her phone for the time. "I'm going to head down to meet Elijah."

"He's not coming up?"

Jeanette's eyes flashed with hurt, but she threw her head into the air, laughing. "Nah. We're past all that. I meet him on the street. He's so busy, you know?" She leaned down and fixed the sling-back on her ultrahigh, black pumps.

"Yeah…" Summer did her best to sound convincing. "I can imagine."

Jeanette smiled at Summer and placed her hand on Summer's cheek. She stroked it, gently. "Men can be real assholes, Sum."

Summer moved to speak, but Jeanette held up her black clutch, stopping her.

"Even if they don't mean to be. That goes for both of them. Elijah and Malcolm. I am positive he's just busy. And whatever it is, is out of his control. I mean, look at you…" Jeanette picked up a piece of Summer's hair and tossed it behind Summer's back. "You're the real deal, gorgeous and brilliant. And if he doesn't appreciate you, well screw 'em."

Jeanette smiled at Summer in a way that made Summer shiver. The way Jeanette said those words, there was no doubt. It—whatever it was with Malcolm—was over.

****

Malcolm paced around his apartment while Winston napped in his dog bed. Winston opened a wary eye, his iris following Malcolm back and forth as Malcolm wore down the polish on his marble floor.

Malcolm got to one end of his massive foyer and immediately turned and walked back the other way.

Winston whimpered.

Malcolm turned to Winston. "Yeah, I know. I know."

Malcolm scratched at his arms, certain his skin was covered in imperceptible bugs. He reached up and rubbed the sweat off his brow, which immediately replenished itself. He tried to take deep breaths to calm his racing heart, but he was unsuccessful. His shoulder blades knit together as a whisper of cold brushed up and down his spine. He placed a hand on his chest, trying to stop the palpitations. If it wasn't that he had experienced an anxiety attack before, he would be convinced he was having a heart attack.

Winston whimpered again and sat up in his bed. He barked.

"I'm okay, boy…" Malcolm fought to keep his breath calm as his pacing became quicker and quicker.

Winston began a low howl, and Malcolm snapped himself around to face Winston.

"Winston, what is it?"

Winston only continued his low guttural growl as Malcolm tried to calm him.

"Shh," Malcolm petted Winston, attempting to soothe the dog, but nothing helped. Winston continued to howl. "Winston, please…"

Malcolm stood up and walked away, feeling heat settle in the base of his spine and climb upward across his chest. He clamped his hands to his ears as Winston's howl cut through his brain, lobotomizing him.

Faster and faster, Malcolm moved until he grew dizzy. The marble suddenly looked very close as he swayed, dangerously close to falling over. Winston howled louder.

"Winston, shut up." Malcolm's voice was sharper than he meant it to be, and Winston growled even louder in response.

Sweat dripped into Malcolm's eyes as he raised a shaking hand, and ran it through his hair. "Winston, please, not tonight."

Winston let out his loudest moan, and Malcolm jumped. He began to sprint, back and forth, trying to run off the demons clutching his throat and chest. Winston wailed.

"Goddamnit, Winston." Malcolm was too loud. He grabbed his own throat, immediately terrified of the damage he may have done. Good. Fuck it. Who gives a crap anyway? How many old musicians fade away, and no one gives a damn? Well, no one should care. Because he wasn't worth it.

Winston moaned again, this time his cry of agony snapped Malcolm into a more lucid state. No, he wasn't worth saving…but Winston sure as hell was.

Malcolm grabbed his cell from his pocket and dropped to a corner of his foyer. The cold marble floor and walls were cool against his burning skin. He lifted a shaking finger. No, he'd never let anyone see him like this—but looking at Winston, Malcolm knew they needed help. Fast. And he knew there was only one person he trusted enough to let help.

"Hello?" Summer answered on the first ring.

"Can you come?" His voice was shaky, and his jaw chattered as he spoke.

"Where are you?" Her voice was serious and determined.

Malcolm choked out his address and hung up the phone. He let his head slump back with a bang against the marble wall, his thoughts drowned out by Winston's howl.

****

Malcolm wasn't sure how long he sat there before his doorman buzzed, but judging by the strength of Winston's persistent howl, it couldn't have been long. Damn it, he should have met Summer downstairs. Carefully, he pulled himself up to his feet, his body trembling, and made his way to his intercom. He lifted the receiver.

"Mr. Angel, sir, there's a girl—"

"Let her up." Malcolm's voice was scratchy, and it hurt to speak. "Clear it with security, and let her through." He leaned against the wall by the side of the door, waiting, his hands shaking so badly he shoved them into his pockets. He knew he looked a mess—

weak and disheveled, but the growing calm in his stomach told him she wouldn't care.

Her knock was forceful and quick.

He pulled open the door, and she stood there looking up at him, her green eyes taking him in, her eyebrows knitted together.

He stepped aside, and she walked in without a single word. Almost immediately, Winston stopped howling. Malcolm stared at her, and they stood facing each other in Malcolm's foyer. Summer surveyed Malcolm's face, studying him, trying to make sense of the mess he was. She took him in without judgment, his disheveled hair, his sweat-stained t-shirt, his eyes red and tired, aching with forbidden tears.

"Have you taken any drugs?" Her voice was monotone.

"No." He shook his head.

"Are you drinking?"

"No." He looked down at the floor between them, embarrassed.

She let out a relieved sigh. "Has this ever happened before?"

"Not like this…"

She nodded as if she understood it all. As if, without speaking, she was somehow able to grasp the pain he was in. Her chest rising and falling quickly, she held out her arms, and he walked to her, falling into her embrace. She leaned up onto her tiptoes and wrapped her arms around his shoulders. She pressed herself against him, tightly. He clung to her, terrified.

Summer dropped to her flatfeet and gently guided Malcolm down to the ground with her. She backed herself up against the door and pulled him to her again.

She readjusted so he leaned his head on her breasts, and that's when the tears began.

Chapter Twelve

Malcolm pressed his head against her, feeling the softness of her sweater and the swell of her breasts, cushioning his pain. Nearly twenty years of repressed feelings began falling out of him, and he saw it before him as if it were all happening again—right now. Malcolm clung to her, wailing into her chest. The louder he wailed, the harder she held him. She never tried to quiet him; never said it was all okay. She just held on.

His dizziness subsided and the itching stopped, but the hard, crushing pain in his chest assured him he was going to die of a heart attack here, against Summer's breast. He gasped for air, clutching at his chest, and immediately she sprung into action.

"Malcolm, can you hear me?"

He nodded a yes.

"You're clutching your chest like you're having a heart attack…we have only five minutes to get you to a hospital."

He grabbed at her arms.

"I understand it's scary, and I know you can't let…" she struggled for the word, "…anyone know, but this is your life. Think, Malcolm. Do you have aspirin in the house?"

He nodded, pointing to the nearest bathroom. She exhaled and slipped him onto his back. His body shaking, he turned his head to watch her run to the bathroom and emerge with a bottle of aspirin. She yanked off the cap and pulled out two pills. She stuffed them into his mouth.

"Chew them. Don't swallow them whole."

Malcolm crushed the pills, choking on the powder and the wretched, bitter taste. She produced a bottle of water from her bag and lifted his head to help him drink.

"Sip, don't gulp."

Malcolm did as she instructed, his shaking beginning to subside, his breathing returning to normal.

"I don't think it's your heart, Malcolm, but we can't take any chances. We need to get you to a hospital."

He shook his head ferociously. She looked off as if considering the options. Her head sprung back quickly.

"You must have a private doctor. Someone who can check you out without anyone know—"

Again Malcolm shook his head. He couldn't be dying. He died seventeen years ago, on this very night. Summer slipped under him and drew his head onto her lap. She stroked his hair, calming him.

"Malcolm, we need to have you looked at…"

Staring up at her, he knew this was his only chance. This would be the only time he could ever admit what had happened.

"I…"

He started convulsing again, and she leaned over him, warming his body with hers.

"I…I killed…"

He felt her breathing quicken.

She held on, looking into his eyes. "Malcolm, did

you do something tonight?"

"No, no…"

Strangely, she stayed. Even when she thought he may have done the unthinkable.

"Sev…seventeen years ago… I…I…Oh, God…" He grabbed at her again and rolled into her. He buried his face in her soft chest.

She held him, stroking his back. "What, Malcolm? Tell me. Let it out."

He pulled back and looked at her, feeling her sincerity, knowing she would take his secret to her grave.

He cleared his throat. "Seventeen years ago, I…I killed someone…"

"Malcolm…" She took his hand.

"It…it was an accident. We were driving…new car." His words were slurred and broken. "A…a convertible." He coughed, and the violent shaking returned. "Two seats. I…I was driving."

"Accidents happen, Malcolm…" Her words were soft.

"No." He shook his head, pulling away. He sat back from her and drew his knee up under him, resting his elbow on it. His eyes darted around the room, like a wild, unbroken bull, harnessed to be ridden. He needed distance…and clarity. He didn't deserve for her to make him feel better. He just needed her to listen.

"The police…they ruled it an accident…" He closed his eyes and breathed deeply. The shaking lessened, but his voice ached to speak. "But I should have known better." He looked off, seeing the airbag deploy, reliving the impact to his head, feeling his muscles strain as he desperately pulled at the boy—

trying to free him from the wreckage and the suffocating air bag. Malcolm looked directly at Summer. "I never should have had a child in that car...I never should have had my child in that car..."

Summer lifted her hand to her mouth, tears springing to her eyes. "Oh, Malcolm." Her words were laced with empathy, but nothing more. "How old was he?" Her voice trembled now, and tears began to roll down her cheeks.

"Almost three." Malcolm clutched his stomach. "Oh, God..."

Again, Summer sprung into action. "Come on."

She was on her feet and guiding him to the bathroom before Malcolm knew what was happening. He felt the color drain from his face, and the bathroom was cold—so cold his shaking grew more and more violent.

"It's...c—cold..." Malcolm fought to say the words through a clenched jaw. He bit down, trying to control his chattering teeth. His stomach clenched, and the muscles in his shoulders and arms tightened. It was nearly impossible to move. He struggled to lift his arm to wipe away the damned sweat, but his arm wouldn't obey. Panic shot up his spine as he fought for a breath. His heart rate raced and dizziness overwhelmed him. His legs began to give out, but Summer helped steady him, wrapping her arm around his waist as he clung to her, his sweat staining her sweater, her own perspiration dripping from her temples.

She held him through the violent seizures and vomiting, until the seventeen years of repressed pain were completely out.

Malcolm fell next to the toilet, his arm draped over

the bowl. He watched as Summer dampened towels and placed them on his forehead and behind his skull, cooling the burning. His eyes leveled on Summer. "I was nineteen when I became a father and twenty-two when I stopped."

She patted the cool cloth on his forehead. "You never stop being a parent, Malcolm. No matter what. It just...changes..." She smiled, sweetly. "That's all."

Her arm was hovering over his head, and he needed...contact. He needed her. He reached up and grabbed her arm with such ferocity, she pulled back, surprised. He gripped her arm tighter, sure she was the only reason he was alive. Without a word she grimaced, and immediately, he lightened his grasp on her. The last thing he wanted was to hurt her.

Still holding her lightly, he drew her arm to him. He pulled her down beside him. They leaned back against the wall, sitting side by side on the cold marble floor of the bathroom.

"How come...how come I've never heard of this?" Summer brushed her hair back from her face as she spoke.

"Because it never existed." His head rolled toward her.

Even here, on the floor of his bathroom, covered in his sweat, stained by his vomit, she was stunning. Her hair was pulled back in a hurried ponytail, and her forehead was creased with worry. Worry about him.

Summer cocked her head. "I'm sorry, I don't understand."

"How could you?" Malcolm squeezed his eyes shut for a moment, letting the pain in his stomach pass. He opened his eyes again, and they found Summer. "I didn't exist then. I had just signed my first contract and gotten my first record deal. That's why the car. His mother wasn't around—took off right after he was born, so it was just us. I thought it'd be cool to take him for a ride." Malcolm's throat ached, his words were laden with anguish. "As soon as I was cleared of all charges, including neglect and child endangerment, my label changed my name."

"You're not really Malcolm Angel?" Summer shook her head, fighting to understand.

"I am, now. It's my legal name. But I was born Angelo Malacad. And Angelo Malacad killed his son…"

"Malcolm…" She sat up and reached out to him, placing her small, warm hands on his cheeks. "It was an accident."

"But I was so stupid…" He looked away, shaking his head.

"You were twenty-two. And you weren't malicious. You didn't plan it. Best I can tell, you were doing everything you could for your son—including spending father and son time together."

"It's not that simple." Malcolm looked away.

"Of course it's not." She placed her warm hands on his arm and then sat back. "Nothing is ever that simple." She crossed her legs under her and eased his head onto her lap. She stroked his hair as she spoke. "What was his name?"

"Julian."

"Like John Lennon's son…"

"Yeah." Malcolm sighed and again the tears poured forth. He wiped them away as he spoke. "I…I've never cried about it. Never once.

People…people just tried to convince me it never happened. And I guess I let them."

She shook her head. "No, you didn't."

He looked up at her.

"And you're crying now."

She smiled so sweetly, Malcolm felt the sob rising in his chest he didn't bother to try to stop. What could it possibly matter now? She had seen it all—she knew all of his secrets. And she was still here, holding him. He cried until he had no more tears to give.

His tears subsided, and she continued to stroke his hair. It calmed him so much; he couldn't ever remember a time when anything ever felt so good.

"That song, Malcolm. The one we've all loved for so many years. Your love song that has been played at all those weddings…it has nothing to do with romantic love…it's about Julian, isn't it?"

"Yeah."

"Yeah."

Summer let her fingers run down his cheeks, scraping against the dark stubble. He stared at her, this angel who sat above him, helping him through the second worst night of his life. He reached up and took her hand, holding it tightly, pulling it to his chest. Then he closed his eyes and there, in his bathroom, his head resting in Summer's lap, he fell into the deepest sleep of his adult life.

****

When Summer woke she looked around, dazed. Malcolm's head was still heavy on her lap, but she needed to text Jeanette to let her know she was okay, and she really needed to pee. But the last thing Summer wanted to do was disturb Malcolm—and how was she going to pee when they were both in the bathroom?

Carefully, she lifted his head and slid out from underneath him. She was sore and stiff from having slept against a marble wall all night. She poked her head out of the bathroom, and Winston reacted to her movements, wagging his tail and whimpering.

"Shh, Winston." She made her way to his bed and petted him. "You need to pee too, huh?" She whispered when she spoke to him.

Winston wagged his tail in response.

"Okay," she smoothed the fur on his back. "Tell you what. I'll run to the bathroom quickly, then I'll take you out, okay?" She glanced back at Malcolm. "It's best just to let him sleep. Any idea for a pillow?"

Winston yelped.

"Shh." Summer glanced around. "There must be a few hundred couches in this place, right? Right."

Summer turned and gaped at Malcolm's living room. She walked past Winston, heading into a living area as big as an arena. "Good grief." The living room had white marble floors, and black leather furniture. A large gray cushion sat opposite the couch, and one entire wall was made of windows, overlooking Central Park, and all of Manhattan.

"Wow…" Summer was momentarily sidetracked by the beauty of the sun rising over Manhattan. She shook her head, focusing, and turned back to the couch. Thankfully, it had tiny throw pillows tucked into the corners. She picked up a pillow that probably cost more than her rent, and brought it back to Malcolm. She leaned down and slipped the pillow under his head. She stood back appraising him. "Better." She looked at Winston. "Now it's my turn." Summer turned around.

"Oh, wait." She saw Malcolm's sleeping body in the bathroom. "Okay Winston, any idea where there's another bathroom?"

Winston wagged his tail.

"Yeah. I figured you weren't talking. Hm..." Summer looked around. "Well, let's leave him a note in case he wakes up and comes looking for you." Summer spun around again, the need to pee escalating. She danced around a bit. "Quickly." She turned around and around, searching. "Okay, if I lived here where would I keep paper?" Summer absolutely refused to snoop or go through drawers, so her search was cursory at best. She gave up, placing her hands on her hips. "Well, we'll text him and hope it doesn't wake him up."

Just as Summer's finger was paused over the 'send' button, she thought of something. She turned to Winston. "Don't you have some fancy dog walker who comes and gets you?"

Winston just wagged again, and Summer giggled, searching for Winston's leash. She'd text Malcolm in a bit, giving him all the undisturbed sleep she could. She turned to Winston.

"Rich people do that, right? They have dog walkers."

"I don't know what most rich people do, but this rich person walks his own dog."

Summer turned, feeling butterflies the size of Giant Swallowtails flutter around her stomach. "Malcolm."

They stared at one another. He looked much better than he had last night. His eyes were red, but there was coloring in his complexion, and the lines on his face were less craterous. He appeared taller and healthier...and frankly, he looked like Malcolm again.

Summer was glad to see it. It just then occurred to her she must look like a disaster—she hadn't so much as peeked into a mirror since she arrived last night. She reached up and ran a hand through her hair.

"I…" She took a deep breath, trying to calm her stutter. "I was just going to walk Winston. I think he needs to pee."

As if on cue, Winston whimpered.

"I'll do that."

Malcolm grabbed the leash, and with a heavy sigh, Summer let go. So that's the way it was going to be. He was going to pretend last night never happened. She couldn't blame him. Well…what mattered was that he was okay. What was she expecting, anyway? It's not like she—

Without a word Malcolm stepped to her and wrapped his arm around her shoulders, pulling her tightly to his chest. She turned her cheek so it rested on his chest, and as he held her, she draped her arms around his back.

Still holding her, he leaned down, planting a single kiss on her forehead.

Chapter Thirteen

After a quick trip to the bathroom to pee and freshen up, they left. It was just the two of them as they walked Winston down Broadway. Apparently, Malcolm was able to go out without security when the city was fairly empty—like now, on a very early Sunday in the middle of summer.

Summer looked up at the sky and smiled. The sun was just waking up, and it promised to shine gloriously today—not too hot—just perfect. She adjusted her oversized glasses it was still too dark to need, and caught Malcolm staring at her shirt.

"What?" She smiled, stuffing her hands into her jeans.

"I like the way my shirt looks on you."

Summer's cheeks warmed. Truth told, Summer loved being in Malcolm's shirt. It was just a plain gray v-neck t-shirt, but it smelled like him. She adored the feel of Malcolm Angel wrapped around her. The v-neck sat perfectly at her top, showing only the tiniest bit of cleavage. The sleeves were much too large, and the shirt hung down to her thighs, but he seemed to like it well enough.

"That's silly…" She waved him off.

"No, really." He reached out and took her hand for a moment, squeezing it. "You look gorgeous."

"Really?" She smirked at him.

"Really. We might have to keep you in my t-shirts—always."

Summer laughed, but burning heat shot from the hand he had squeezed up through her arm, resulting in her face flushing. She fanned herself, racking her brain for the plausible reason for this sudden hot flash. Medically, it could be the stress hormones epinephrine or norepinephrine, but she wasn't feeling a bit stressed. If anything, she was feeling quite calmly content. Think, think, think. There had to be a reason she was feeling this rush, this warmth all over—a hypothalamus dysfunction? She should be so lucky. There was only one answer that could explain her sudden perspiration, and he was about six feet tall with the body of a god and the voice of an angel…Malcolm Angel. The aroma of warm bagels caught her attention, offering a reprieve from her thoughts, and she threw her small nose up into the air, sniffing. Winston barked.

"Right, Winston? Bagels. They smell incredible."

"The store over there—across the street—specializes in them." Malcolm pointed to an orange and white awning. "Best in the world."

"Best bagels in the world?" Summer turned to him, lifting her glasses, her eyes wide. "Let's go." Letting her glasses drop, she grabbed his arm and started pulling.

He laughed. "Hold on a sec. I haven't eaten a bagel in…I don't know how long." Malcolm stood still, shaking his head.

"Why not?" They stopped under a tree, and Summer smiled. She would never have guessed in the middle of all the concrete and high rises, there could be life. "If I lived here I'd eat them every day. At least every Sunday."

"Are you gonna?" He turned to Summer. The intensity of his words hung like fog between them, cooling her burning skin, and blanketing the nearly deserted street.

"Am I going to what?" She stared at the ground, shifting her weight from foot to foot.

"Live here." He turned his head away and then back. "Is that your plan?"

Summer stared at Malcolm, feeling his vulnerability.

"I—I don't know what my plan is." She mumbled her words, her stomach seizing. She gazed up at him, knowing she should tell him the truth—she had a very definite plan that began right after Labor Day. And that plan would take her far from New York City—for good. He deserved to know, but she was terrified if she confessed, everything would change. And besides, the vulnerability he was exhibiting this morning was only because of last night. The ache in her eyes confirmed that. Once Malcolm was feeling like himself again, he would move on from Summer to some bone-thin supermodel who was tempting him with her swimsuit body and not warm bagels. No doubt about that. Summer sighed, petrified the slightest slip of the lip would drive Malcolm away prematurely, and for good… And heaven knows, she wasn't ready for either of those options.

Malcolm smiled. "So whaddaya say we grab some bagels? I'm famished."

"I can imagine…" Summer squeezed her eyes shut. She shook her head, mentally kicking herself. She swore to herself she was not going to bring up last night. He certainly didn't need to relive it.

"Sum…"

The use of her nickname gave her a definite pull toward him, and she turned her entire body to face him. The early morning sun relaxed her as she looked up at him.

"It's okay." He reached out and placed his hand on her cheek. He stroked it gently and then pulled back, smiling. "You don't have to skirt around the subject. Actually…I…I owe you an explanation. And a thank you."

Summer settled her eyes on him. "You owe me nothing, Malcolm. I was there because I wanted to be."

"I'm glad you were."

"Me too."

"But still, Summer…"

Summer let her eyes linger, heavy on Malcolm. She sighed, scratching a phantom itch on her arm. She took a deep breath before speaking.

"When I was sixteen, my parents begged me to go to a Memorial Day picnic with them. I had just gotten my license, and the picnic was just about the last thing I wanted to do. I didn't want to hang around a bunch of middle aged people, sipping chardonnay, and discussing politics. I was a really good student, and I deserved a break. I deserved to have some fun with my friends."

"Jeanette?"

"Yup." Summer looked away, her eyes aching. Her voice remained strong as she fought through the tears. "I was with Jeanette when I got the call. The police officers called her house…her parents were my emergency contact and mine, hers. They tracked down the number that way." Summer scoffed. "You know what's so odd?"

"What's that?" He didn't touch her, and she knew he was giving her space while she spoke.

"I can still smell the room I was in when I got the call. The house was engulfed with that certain…sweet but sultry smell of blueberries cooking in the oven. Jeanette was arguing with her mom, because her mom was trying to get us to eat some pie to celebrate Memorial Day. Of course Jeanette was always on a diet so she said no, but I passed as well—though I wasn't sure why. I'm an eater…" Summer smiled when she said this, laughing a half-hearted laugh. "And normally, I like pie, but that day…as soon as I smelled the blueberries on that day, something hit me in the stomach. Something was wrong." She tucked her hair behind her ears and cleared her throat. "To this day I don't eat blueberries."

Summer raised her shoulders and dropped them, hard.

"But you weren't responsible, Sum."

"Wasn't I?" Buried behind the thick, black lens, her eyes made their way to his. "They asked me to go. I had just gotten my license. I wouldn't have had anything to drink at the picnic…maybe if I had driven home, they'd still be alive…"

"You can't know that." Malcolm stroked her arm.

"Nope. But I screamed, 'I hate you!' at them before they left that day. And I *can* know that is the biggest regret of my life."

"Summer…" Malcolm's voice was sweet.

"And you know what my mother said back to me?"

Malcolm shook his head, his body leaning toward

hers, his arms waiting to embrace her, and Summer knew he wanted nothing more than to make her pain go away—just as she had wanted to do for him.

"She said…" Summer bit the corner of her lip, fighting the tears. "She said, 'I'm sorry you hate me right now. But I love you. And always will. No matter what.' And I just huffed and stormed away." Summer's voice was a whisper. She reached up and wiped away a tear. She spoke through a cracking voice. "And the irony of it all was I was normally such a good kid. It was the first time I had ever acted like that." She shook her head, gazing at Malcolm. "Timing's everything, isn't it?"

He reached out and took her hand.

"Malcolm," Summer squeezed his hand. "I didn't tell you this to try to compete with you. There's nothing worse than the loss of a child. That's…" She took a deep breath and let it out, audibly. "That's unthinkable. I told you my story so you'd understand…you're not alone."

"Summer…" Malcolm pulled off his glasses and slipped hers off as well. He stared into her eyes, eyes that were red with worry and exhaustion. "I don't feel alone anymore. I…I haven't since the day I met you."

Summer inhaled sharply, looking up into Malcolm's eyes. His sincerity bore a hole straight through her, letting whatever decency there was left in her spill out onto the street. How could she mislead him like this? But it was too late now…the time to tell him the truth was weeks ago. Now, if she was lucky enough to be with him, she'd have to wait to tell him the truth until summer ended. When summer ends, she would explain everything. Until then…

Malcolm stepped toward Summer and wrapped his arm around her waist. He looked at her with eyes so hungry and lost, she needed to look away. She ran her tongue over her teeth, feeling the minty grit left from the quick finger brushing she did before they took Winston out. Malcolm's incredibly broad shoulders, and strong, sinewy arms, protected her from all the pain she had felt only moments before. Somehow, seeing behind the rock star persona to the man he really was—made him all the more desirable.

"Malcolm, I…"

He placed his hand under her chin, guiding her face back toward his. He eased his hands up onto either side of her face, and held her…his grasp intense. She closed her eyes, her breath racing, her breasts pushing against his chest as he leaned down and ever-so-gently, brushed his lips against hers.

Chapter Fourteen

"I don't wanna let you go, today…" Malcolm's words were a whisper in her ear.

"Then don't." Her eyes were still closed, and she snuggled further into Malcolm's embrace, with Winston waiting patiently at their feet.

"Come home with me."

The tiny blonde hairs on her arms bristled…his words, pure seduction. Her nipples hardened in response to his earthy, scratchy voice…the voice she had heard croon out maybe hundreds of love songs. And now that voice was uttering words meant only for her.

"Summer?" He held her a slight distance from him. "Sum?"

His arms muscles tensed—she needed to answer him. Her breathing increased, rapidly. For the past few weeks she had wanted nothing more than to be with Malcolm…alone…in that way. But now that it was here, could she handle it?

She nodded, unable to form words.

"Summer…" He chuckled when he spoke. "Is that a yes?"

The way he spoke—his deep, paced voice—made her feel as much like a child as it did a woman. Looking up at him, she knew he would be completely and irrevocably in charge. Her pulse throbbed in her temples, a warm flush climbed up into her cheeks, and she wiped her sweaty palms on her jeans. Her sympathetic nervous system was in overdrive…and she didn't blame it one bit. Good grief…she wanted this.

"Oh, wait…" She shook her head as gosh darn reality dashed in and stomped its oversized boots all over her blissful thoughts. She pulled back.

"I don't think I like where this is going, Summer…"

He ran his hands up and down her arms, his head bowed to look into her eyes. She nearly swooned.

"It—I…" How exactly does one form a sentence while Malcolm Angel holds you like you're the one present he's always wanted? "I…I just, I have to stop home. I need to get some things…" If she was finally going to be with Malcolm—in whatever capacity—she wanted to make sure she grabbed a shower and had clean underwear. She felt her cheeks heat.

Malcolm smirked at her, holding up his forefinger. "Wait a sec…"

He reached into the pocket of his jeans, grinning when there suddenly wasn't enough room for his hand. Summer bit her lip and looked away. He texted quickly, smiling at a response.

"There." He shoved the cell back into his pocket.

"What's there?" Summer was confused.

"I'm having some stuff delivered for you."

"Some stuff?"

"Toothbrush, that kind of thing."

"Oh…uh…okay…"

"And I sent a messenger to Jeanette's. Jeanette said she'd get some of your things together. Clean shorts, etc… As far as shirts go, I think we've got that covered."

He winked, and Summer's stomach flipped. Holy cow.

"You got all that done just now?"

He shrugged, grinning. "There are some perks to being me." He pulled her closer to him. "Like, right now, for example."

He smiled a wide, generous smile, and Summer smiled back.

****

When Malcolm let her into his apartment it was like Summer had never before been there. She had been so focused last night, she had barely noticed her surroundings.

They crossed the massive foyer and walked toward the kitchen. Malcolm set down the bag of warm bagels on the counter. "Ready for the tour?"

"Mm-hm…" She nodded, lingering outside the kitchen, trying to suppress a giggle.

"What are you giggling about?"

"Nothing." She pursed her lips, fighting her smile, looking over the kitchen of stark white and silver.

"You can come in, nothing in here bites."

"Are you sure?" She entered cautiously. "Malcolm, I don't want to tell you your business, but you may have been had when you purchased your apartment. You might want to give your real estate agent a call."

"Why's that?"

He grinned as she spoke.

"Well, I hate to be the one to tell you, but you have no appliances. No dishwasher, no refrigerator…no microwave…no anything." She spun around in a circle.

"Here, smart ass." He pulled open a wall and

miraculously, a fridge appeared.

"Are you kidding me?" Summer moved over to stand next to Malcolm. She stared into the well stocked fridge. "There are secret doors and panels? If I get stuck behind one, should I ask you to, 'Put the candle back...'?"

"Very funny. We'll keep you on this side of the hidden door just to be safe. And they're not secret—just unobtrusive."

"Knowing where you refrigerator is, is obtrusive?"

Malcolm laughed. "Well, when you say it like that... But c'mon. It's cool, huh?"

"Yeah, I guess. I think I saw this on an episode of the Jetsons once. Was that your favorite show growing up?"

"One of them."

"I'll bet." She looked down for a minute, then back to him. "Where did you grow up?"

"Detroit." He barely moved, his eyes fixed on her.

She chewed her lip, terrified she was overstepping a boundary, but she asked anyway. "City raised?"

"Yup. A rundown part of the city, held together by a bandage. We did not have unobtrusive appliances. Actually, we were lucky we had appliances at all. No dishwasher. No microwave. But we did have a fridge."

She nodded, staring at his face—seeing the city etched into every line. "Your, uh... parents?"

He shook his head. "Just my mom."

"She must be incredibly proud."

"She was..."

"Oh..." Summer's shoulders slumped forward again. "I'm sorry, Malcolm."

"It happens. After awhile...they all just begin to

pile up, cushioning one another, so the higher the pile, the softer the blow—the less you feel."

"Like the Princess and the Pea."

"I guess."

"But the princess felt the pain. No matter how many mattresses there were."

"That's the irony of it all, isn't it?" He reached up and grabbed the back of his neck with his hand.

She studied his face, wondering…wishing she could make his pain go away, if only for a moment.

He nodded to her. "How 'bout you? Where'd you grow up?"

"Connecticut."

"Figures."

"Hey." She crossed her arms in front of her chest. "Have I just been insulted?"

"Guess that depends on your feelings toward Connecticut."

"And yours?"

He just grinned at her, and she smirked in return. She walked past Malcolm, running her hand along a sparkling countertop similar to Jeanette's.

"Nice…quartz?"

"Good guess. Enameled lava stone." The smile in his eyes dared her.

Summer laughed, tossing her head. "Really? This just gets better and better. That's a thing?"

"Yup. A really, stupidly expensive thing."

"Explains why I've never heard of it."

His eyes locked on hers, and she saw something flash through them. Suddenly, she felt so incredibly sad for him. Her shoulders dropped, and she leaned back against the enameled lava.

"Must stink to be you sometimes."

He raised his eyebrows. "Yeah? Why?"

"Wondering if a woman is here because you're you, because you're famous, or..." she couldn't stifle the giggle, "because you have enameled lava stone countertops."

He nodded and crossed his arms, leaning back against the countertop. "Yeah, sometimes."

He adapted his cocky rock star pose, but she could tell underneath he was just the tiniest bit vulnerable.

Summer walked to him, still smiling. "Well, let me assure you, whatever you show me here in this apartment, will be lost on me. I will 'ooo' and 'ahhh' at all appropriate times, but I've got no clue what I'm looking at. This is so far removed from my world..." She shook her head again, snickering. "So if I'm here, I promise you it's because of you...and Winston."

He beamed at her.

"All right, get on with it. Show me some more stuff I will not have the ability to fully appreciate."

"Right this way..." He held out his arm, and Summer followed him to another room.

****

"I was wrong..." Summer's voice was a mere whisper.

They stood side by side, before a giant, angular soaking tub, staring out a window with a breathtaking view of Manhattan.

"Can you see the entire city?" Summer continued to whisper, though she wasn't sure why.

"Well, Uptown, Downtown, the East Side and some of Queens."

"My goodness. All while you soak in a tub?"

They stood quietly for a moment, and then Summer turned her head toward him.

"You love these city views, don't you?"

"I guess."

She gazed back out the window. "You took me to that old hotel for the view…and your apartment…you have views from every room."

"Yeah."

"And the higher up the better."

Malcolm continued to stare out the window, nodding. He swallowed hard. Summer took a deep breath, turning to him. She spoke softly.

"Does it feel better? Being closer to him?"

Malcolm slipped his hand in hers. "The only time I ever feel better is when I'm with you…"

****

He felt her gasp before he heard it. He was certain he could feel everything in Summer before she ever expressed it. He had such a connection to her, one that never existed with anyone else…ever. He looked at her standing there: her wavy, blonde hair falling down her back, her perfect profile, the swell of her breasts, and dip of her tummy. God, she was beautiful. And smart. She was so unaffected by the trivialities of life—it was like she understood some greater purpose. Malcolm smiled a crooked smile, hoping she would teach him one day.

She squeezed his hand, understanding him.

Above all, Malcolm trusted her. Trust. That's what it all boiled down to. Summer was the first person he honestly felt he could trust, in…maybe ever.

Malcolm swallowed the lump in his throat, because no matter what…no matter how he felt, he didn't deserve her and couldn't be with her past this summer. These few weeks were already longer than he ever planned to be with her. It was longer than he'd ever been with anyone. It was longer than he should have stayed. Once summer ended, he'd have to end it.

"Could I..." Her words were a struggle.

He smiled. She was shy. He knew from the moment he saw her onstage she wasn't an experienced groupie who followed bands professionally.

"Wanna grab a shower?"

She nodded, grateful.

"C'mon."

He led her to a bath just down the hall from the master, offering her privacy.

"Am I going to be able to work the shower?" She tried her best to remain playful, but her lip quivered when she spoke, and her voice was soft.

"Ha, ha." He smiled, trying to relieve her tension. The last thing he wanted was for her to be nervous. He had been waiting for her a long, long time, and as he stared at her, gorgeous and vulnerable, he was eternally grateful he had.

He left her with towels and all the bags and supplies Jeanette had sent. He was always amazed at how many products women used, especially when they looked their most beautiful without a speck of makeup, and wearing his shirt. Or, at least, that's how Summer looked her most beautiful.

He made his way back to the master suite. After grabbing a quick shower himself, he dressed and sat on the edge of his bed, inhaling deeply...thinking of her in the shower. He imagined the warm water from his rain shower head falling down on her hair, her head thrown back, eyes closed. He could see the tiny bumps on her perfectly toned arms and shoulders as water spattered her round, full breasts—splashing against her nipples…cherry red and hard…then slipping between her breasts, running down her cleavage… sliding down the contour of her belly…passing between her legs, before it continued its descent down her thighs…

Damn. He stood up, pacing the room. He shoved his hands into his pockets, counting upwards by threes. Maybe when he reached the millions he would calm down.

Water from his shower, spraying her tight nipples…Ugh…Malcolm clenched his teeth, certain they could tear through Kevlar given the chance. He didn't want Kevlar, he wanted those perfectly ripe buds in his mouth to lick and suck until she cried out in ecstasy.

How long can a shower take? Malcolm turned his wrist to check his watch. She'd only been in there ten minutes. He'd have at least another fifty to go. No woman could ever get ready for anything in less than an hour, right?

His eyes made their way to his bedroom door. He wanted her…needed her…now. He paced to the door—should he go get her? Drag her out of the shower and hold her, dripping wet, against the tile of the bathroom wall, his mouth locked on hers, her legs wrapped around his waist? His hands supporting her perfectly shaped backside…

No. No. No. Not for their first time. Malcolm dragged his hands up through his hair. What the hell was he thinking? Their first time…? Would there be more times? Not at this rate, if he finished before she ever started.

Calm down, Malcolm. So what if her body is everything female, making him feel entirely male...? And who cares if her eyes are so profound they're the color of the sincerest night...? Oh wait. Shit.

Malcolm grabbed a notepad from his side table and began jotting the lyrics. He hadn't written a song about a particular woman...*for* a particular woman...ever. He stared at the line, humming an easy melody. It worked. His heart rate increased and sweat broke out across his forehead. What the hell was he doing?

He tore the paper out of his notebook and crumpled it. No way. He wasn't about to start now. Malcolm Angel made his fortune by squelching his pain—he had no right to be happy. No matter how Summer Wynters made him feel.

He plopped on the bed, running his hands down his thighs. She would be here soon—in his bedroom. What should he do? The usual pattern of champagne and sex on the couch was out of the question...Summer deserved so much more. But why? Because this was going to be her thank you for last night? Did he think he was that good in bed? Was he beginning to believe his own hype? Damn it... What the hell was wrong with him?

Malcolm stared at the bedroom door again, just like Winston when he needed to go out to take a leak. Thankfully, Winston was asleep in his bed in the hall—he didn't need to witness Malcolm acting like such an uncool idiot.

Where was she? Thirteen minutes. Man. He might as well be back in high school. What would she be wearing when she made her way back to him? He really hoped she would be in the clean t-shirt he set out for her, and not some fancy lacy getup Jeanette packed. He stood back up, uncomfortable. Damn, he hadn't been this out of control since he was a kid. He jumped up and down, like he was prepping for stage, and his eyes landed on the master bath. He stuffed his hand into his jeans, feeling the pressure, and seriously contemplated taking matters into his own hand—just so he could be sure to last as long as Summer wanted.

He chuckled, shaking his head. Just then, she pushed the door open and came inside.

Chapter Fifteen

Malcolm's breath hitched. "My God, you are so beautiful."

She stood by the doorway, her back against the wall, her legs popping out of her t-shirt.

She scoffed, smiling. "I—I wasn't sure what to put on. But I figured you lent me the shirt for a reason, and truthfully, I kind of really like wearing it."

His eyes dropped from hers to the v-neck of her shirt, and then traveled farther down. Her nipples were hard, poking through his shirt. She could feel his eyes on her, he knew it, but instead of shrinking back, she inhaled deeply, allowing her chest to rise up and down. He wanted to walk to her and hold her in a tight cocoon against the wall, but he just couldn't stop staring—at any, and all, parts of her. She had no makeup on her face, and her hair was freshly washed and still damp.

She looked down and chewed her lip. "Um, is everything okay?"

He nodded, moving toward her. He paced himself, certain if he moved too fast she would shy away, and he would combust.

"Do you have any idea how gorgeous you are?"

Her eyes climbed up to his, and she shook her head.

He stood in front of her and reached out to stroke her face, softly. "Your face..." He touched her hair.

"Your hair…" He let his hands drop down her arms, his hands engulfing hers. "Your body…"

He moved closer, pushing her back against the wall with his hips.

"Huh…" She let out a guttural moan as she made contact with the wall.

His hands cupped her cheeks, and she stared at him, her giant eyes, aching. He wanted her right now—he wanted *in* her—now, against this wall. He wanted to bury himself so far into her, he could forget who he was…he wanted to touch her in ways no man had ever touched her…and no man ever would again.

But that wasn't his to do…and she wasn't his to keep.

Aw, fuck it.

Malcolm pushed against her, his kiss so forceful she grunted into his mouth. Her mouth opened willingly, and his tongue found its way in—every part of his body needing to claim her. He wanted her—on her, in her—he wanted her in ways he had never before wanted a woman…

He pushed harder against her, and she moaned. With his mouth still on hers, he pulled his body back and grabbed his t-shirt. He broke his kiss only to rip off his shirt. Staring at his chest, her eyes widened, then they wandered down, landing on his waistband…she reached out and traced his tattoo of a fallen angel.

"Like it?" His words were a breathless growl.

She nodded, biting her lip that was already puffy from his kiss. Her hand made its way to her mouth, tracing her swollen lips.

Malcolm breathed deeply—if she thinks that's swollen…Just wait…

In an instant Malcolm was latched back onto her, his bare chest feeling the softness of the cotton of her shirt, and the stiffness of her nipples. Oh, those nipples...nipples he had been fantasizing about for...

He took Summer's arms and planted them over her head, holding her against the wall. Her kiss intensified, and she pushed against him, unable to move. He kissed her now like a hungry fire, devouring her oxygen...growing and intensifying with every second that passed.

He felt her succumb to his strength, exciting him beyond anything he had ever known. He let her arms go, grabbing her t-shirt. Carefully but quickly, he lifted it over her head and tossed it on the ground beside them. He stood back from her—looking. Her breasts were even more beautiful than he had imagined—large and full and shaped like teardrops—her nipples, cherry red as he had guessed—hard and stiff. His eyes scanned her up and down—not a mark, not a blemish—not a single tattoo in sight. He inhaled sharply...could this be possible?

"No tattoos?"

She shook her head. "Is—is that okay?"

Oh, it was more than okay. His eyes raced up and down her body, inspecting every square inch of her unblemished perfection. He wanted to see it all, and do, even more... "Yes, Summer...it's more than okay...it's perfect."

"Malcolm..." Her voice was breathy, and she rolled her head toward him as she spoke.

That was it. Malcolm dropped to his knees before her, his mouth latching on to her nipple, his hands, cupping her breasts.

"Malcolm…" she repeated his name, her hands tightening into fists, grabbing his hair.

With every moan, he grew more and more excited. He moved expertly from nipple to nipple, while her panties—light pink, with only the tiniest bit of lace—were right there, in front of him. She crossed her legs, rubbing them together. He couldn't take anymore.

In one movement, Malcolm stood and lifted her, wrapping her legs around his waist. She groaned in response, and he could feel the moistness from her panties against his abdomen. He kissed her while he held her, his jeans growing tighter and tighter. She weighed nothing, and he carried her to his bed, easily.

He planted one knee on the bed and laid her back. His arms were still wrapped around her as he leaned down over her. He loved the feeling of being on top of her—his wide chest and back covering her completely. Her eyes rolled into her head as he pressed against her.

"Oh…" She gasped, her legs tightening around his waist as she rubbed herself against him. "Malcolm…"

Under usual circumstances, they'd both be naked by now, and he would have already penetrated her. But he wanted to take his time with Summer, as much as his body would allow him to, anyway. Normally, he wouldn't have cared all that much about the woman he was with…but with Summer, he wanted to make this unforgettable.

"I've got you, baby…" He whispered into her ear as he slid himself off of her, and lay by her side. He slipped his hand down into her panties, feeling the incredible warmth and wetness—desperate to climb into both.

She grabbed the blankets into her fists as slowly,

his finger pushed its way in.

"Huh…" Tiny bumps formed all over her body, and her back arched—responses to his touch. Her reactions were so immediate it drove him wild. Carefully, he pushed in a second finger.

"Summer, you're so tight…"

"Too tight?" She spoke through a haze.

"No, baby…" He shook his head, smiling at her.

He didn't bother to wonder what positions she'd like best—he could feel it. Feel her. Malcolm stood up and slipped off his jeans, grabbing himself.

Her eyes widened, and she turned her head, covering her mouth with her hand. "Malcolm…I…"

He reached around to the side table and snatched a condom. He tore the wrapper in his teeth, spitting the broken piece to the floor. With one hand, he unrolled the condom onto himself, and then climbed onto the bed, holding himself above her.

Her eyes closed as he leaned down over her. She reached out tentatively and touched him, pulling away almost immediately. He took her hand and guided her back, showing her how to grasp him. He inhaled sharply—her warm hand feeling better than any drug he had ever taken or thrill he had ever chased. She placed both hands on him, and Malcolm sighed. She felt too good.

He balanced on one arm as he took her hands and moved them to his shoulders. He smiled, leaning down closer to her, hearing her gasp.

"Nervous?" He brushed his forehead against hers.

She shook her head, but he knew better.

"You have nothing to be nervous about."

"I—I don't know if I can handle…"

"We'll take it slow, okay?"

She nodded.

"I promise you...I would never hurt you." And deep inside, Malcolm knew he never would. She meant too much to him.

He began to push his way in. She was tight—incredibly tight—but so hot and wet. She moaned with every inch he claimed, making it so freaking hard to stay calm. Deeper he pushed, and her hands gripped his shoulders. With one final thrust he was in as far as she could take him...

"Oh, God, Malcolm..." Her chest rose up to meet his.

Suddenly, all Malcolm wanted was to stay inside her, forever. He dropped to his forearms, cradling her face with his hands, purposely slowing them both down. He kissed her, over and over, her mouth rising to his. He slid in and out slowly, moving carefully, making sure she felt him in every part of her—fighting his urge to take her in a million different ways.

She gripped his shoulders, and sweat formed between their bodies. He loved the feel of her naked body against his—of her surrendering to his strength and size.

Everything was up to him right now. Everything.

"Malcolm...I..."

Her nails scratched against his back, and he knew she was close. He pressed down, leaning against her, covering her mouth with his. She moaned into his mouth as she rubbed against him. He inhaled, feeling her tightening. She pushed harder still, grabbing his hips, pulling him to her. Finally, she released, moans flooding the room, her body convulsing under his. And it was the sexiest thing he had ever experienced…

He couldn't hold back. He thrust harder against her, the sound of her tiny gasps, filling his empty soul. He drove harder and farther still, until finally, he groaned a deep, guttural groan, letting go. Still supporting his weight, he fell, sweaty and exhausted, on top of Summer.

Deep inside Summer, Malcolm finally understood what it meant to be a man.

****

She felt the single tear escape and reached up to wipe it away before he saw it. Too late. He pulled back, stroking her cheek, studying her.

"You okay?"

"Mmm…" She smiled, choking back tears that were threatening to ruin everything. She tried desperately to put her completely irrational emotions into perspective. It was a release, that's all…an incredible, life-altering release, caused by Malcolm Angel. "I'm just being stupid."

"Hey…"

The intimacy of having Malcolm still inside her was mind-numbing.

"Tell me…" His voice was sweet, and quiet. He stroked her cheek again. "I have never known you to be stupid."

They both smiled.

"So what, you're not happy?"

The worry etched into his brow made her speak more quickly than she meant. "It's just a release. Sorry. I—I haven't let go like that…in…well, ever…"

"Aw, c'mon. I find that hard to believe." He was still on top of her, kissing her softly as he spoke.

She pressed her lips together, sighing. All of it—the idea of only one time with Malcolm, the thought of leaving him in a few minutes, the reality of moving away forever—all of it was too awful.

"Sum?" He pulled up, staring into her eyes.

She felt braver. "If you're asking if I've ever had my world rocked like that before, the answer is a resounding 'no'."

"Really?" He was wearing a giant smirk.

"Really."

He leaned down, pressing his head to hers. "How close have you come?"

She giggled and felt him move slightly. "Oh, sorry." She giggled again, covering her mouth. "I'm not trying to kick you out."

"I know."

He closed his eyes as he said these words, and the way he said them, so confident and sexy…Summer felt her breathing increase as a very definite swell surrounded him again.

"So? Summer?"

"Seriously?" She tilted her head, trying to read him.

"Yeah."

She heard the vulnerability in him.

"Okay. First tell me why it's so important to you."

He nodded. "I am one of the wealthiest men in the world. I am an international success with diamond and multi-platinum albums, and tons of screaming fans worldwide. I've been on top of my game for so many years, it's estimated my overall sales will dwarf The Beatles. The. Beatles. So yeah, I'm fiercely competitive about everything I want…and everything I care about."

Summer stared, dumbstruck, as she felt him grow harder again. Was he telling her not only did he want her, he also cared for her? Both his cockiness and his self-assurance were so incredibly hot. She chewed her lip.

"C'mon. Leave that poor lip to me, and fess up. Tell me, before me, how close have you come to having your world 'rocked'...to use your word. Although I would have used another."

Although his tone was playful, Summer's nipples grew even harder, and that certain pull started in her chest and radiated downward, surrounding him. He shifted then, and she knew he could sense it.

"Never. I've never had my world rocked." She looked down. "I've never had an experience anything like that. I only had one boyfriend..." She squeezed her eyes shut, terrified she may have blown everything by the use of the word, 'boyfriend.' She had to make Malcolm understand she didn't expect him to be her boyfriend. "And until today, he was the only man I'd ever..."

"Wait. No way." Malcolm pulled himself up. "You've only been with one other man before me?"

"There was a boy in high school, but he really wasn't anything."

Malcolm grinned at her.

"Why are you grinning?"

He thrust forward, incredibly hard once again.

She gripped the sheets, gasping. "How...how does that happen so fast?"

He smiled.

"Well, uh...your turn..." Summer rolled her head back as she tried to form words. "What word you would have used? To describe this?"

He thrust, and she inhaled sharply.

"You said…"

He thrust harder, and she caught her breath.

"I know what I said. I'll tell you under one condition."

"Yes?" Her eyes were closed, and she moved with him, losing her battle with consciousness.

"You come on tour with me."

"What?" Summer's breath was choppy, and she shook her head, fighting for clarity.

"Do we have a deal? You come on tour with me—this leg of the tour is short. East coast, Miami, then back up. We're playing the Garden again for Labor Day. Big finish." He drove harder with the words, 'big finish.'

"I…uh…"

"Say yes, Summer…" He leaned down by her ear, whispering. "Say you'll come on tour with me, and I'll tell you."

She held her breath and let it go. "Y—yes."

He exhaled, and stopped his movement, cradling her face in his hands. He gazed directly into her eyes. "I would have said I made love to you."

She lifted her mouth to his.

Chapter Sixteen

"Are you mad at me?" Summer sat crossed legged on Jeanette's couch. She pulled a pillow onto her lap and held her arms tightly. Her bags were packed and waiting by the door.

"Of course not." Jeanette forced a smile. "I'm just surprised you're going…" She looked off.

"Is there some reason I shouldn't?"

Jeanette shook her head.

Summer moved closer to her friend. "Jean. This is me. Tell me the truth. Are you disappointed in me for doing this?"

"What?" Jeanette's eyes fell on Summer. "Of course not, Summer. I'm thrilled for you. Thrilled. Really. No one deserves to have a good time more than you."

Summer flinched. "A good time?" There was something in the way Jeanette said those words.

Jeanette whipped around to face Summer, her hair gliding over her shoulders. "That is why you're going, right? I mean my smart, logical friend doesn't think she and Malcolm Angel are in love, does she?"

Summer narrowed her eyes. "Of course not."

"Good. Because I'd hate to see all that scientific training fly out the window after spending one night with a sexy, dark-haired, bad boy. And he is a bad boy. You know that, right?"

157

"He's a nice person…" Summer spoke into the floor, unable to face Jeanette.

Jeanette laughed, slapping her leg. "Oh, you have to be kidding me. You think you know Malcolm better than anyone now?"

Summer shook her head, swallowing hard. What she knew about Malcolm she would take to her grave.

"And what about him? Does he know you?"

Summer shrugged.

"Oh, really? Then tell me, what does he think about the fact that you're a vet?"

Summer looked off.

"Summer?" Jeanette leaned forward, her eyes flashing.

"He doesn't know." Summer's voice was a whisper, and she bit the inside of her cheek.

"Ohhhh," Jeanette exaggerated her words, nodding. "He doesn't know. Probably the most important thing in your life, but you forgot to mention this to your rock and roll, nice guy boyfriend."

"He's not my boyfriend." Summer stared at Jeanette.

"Damn right, he's not." Jeanette stood with a huff.

"Stop being so nasty, Jeanette." Summer jumped in front of Jeanette, confronting her. "What is it…? I thought you'd be glad you'd have me to sit with at the concerts and—"

"I'm not going, Summer."

"What?" Summer squinted, trying to understand. "Of course you're going. Malcolm said Elijah was traveling with—"

"Malcolm said, huh?"

Jeanette raised her eyebrows in the most

condescending way, and Summer fought to take a deep breath.

Jeanette crossed her arms, and looked down her nose at Summer. "Well, Malcolm was right…this time. Elijah's going. I'm not." Jeanette took off out of the room.

Summer knew exactly where Jeanette was heading. She followed Jeanette down the hall into the half bath. Summer stood in the doorway with her hands stuffed into the pockets of her jeans. "Let me guess, you're not thin enough? Good grief, Jean. You're like a hundred pounds and five foot ten." Summer felt the exasperation climbing up her.

"I'm a hundred and five." Jeanette stepped off the scale.

"You know that's not healthy, right?" Summer refused to move, trapping Jeanette in the bathroom. "Jean, your body won't last forever at that weight. Your skin will show it, your hair…"

"Some of us aren't naturally beautiful, Summer. What can I say?" Jeanette splashed water on her face.

"What are you talking about?" Summer's voice rose. "Why are you mad at me? I weigh plenty more than a hundred and five pounds, and you know it. And I'm four inches shorter than you. Cut the crap, Jeanette."

"Cut the crap?" Jeanette wheeled around, dabbing her face with a towel. "Oh, now we speak like him, too?"

Jeanette pushed her way past Summer and into the living room. Summer followed.

"What the hell, Jean? Why are you being so incredibly nasty to me? Why don't you eat something?

Maybe you'll be in a better mood."

"Because it's not fair." Jeanette stomped her foot as she spoke.

"What's not?"

"This is the only life I have ever wanted, and you're living it."

Summer stepped back. "Do you want to be with Malcolm?"

Jeanette waved her off. "Of course not. I wanted a relationship. That's why I went for Elijah. I figured…"

She looked down, and Summer could hear the pain in her voice.

Jeanette took a deep breath, lifting her head. "I figured a not-so-great looking middle-aged guy would consider himself incredibly lucky to be with me. I thought I'd have my prince—who'd treat me like a princess. Every time I kiss him it's like kissing Rocko all over again."

Summer shook her head. "I'm sorry, Jean. Are you sure you want this?"

"Of course I want it."

"Well maybe, maybe he's just going to be incredibly busy on the trip and doesn't want you to be bored?"

Jeanette stared at Summer, shaking her head. "You are so naïve, Summer."

Summer furrowed her brows. "Jean—"

"And it's a tour, Summer. Not a trip." Jeanette shook her head, walking past Summer. She grabbed her bag and a jacket.

"It's ninety degrees out there."

"I'm chilly." Jeanette pulled her jacket on and sauntered to the door, purposely stepping around

Summer's bags. "Enjoy your *trip*, Summer." Her eyes leveled on Summer. "And I'd appreciate it if you would get the rest of your things out of here just as soon as you get back."

"Jeanette—?"

"Why don't you move in with your billionaire, nice guy rock star who only you can understand?" Jeanette slammed the door.

****

Although Summer felt awful about her argument with Jeanette, it was incredibly easy to get swept up in being with Malcolm. Within a day on the road, Malcolm was gearing up for his next performance.

"Here's how it'll work." He leaned over in his seat, holding her hand tightly between them. She used her free hand to pet Winston, while Malcolm turned her hand slowly in his, staring at it. "We hit Philly in a couple of hours. Daytime the band'll travel with us, we need to work. I've got some new stuff to try out. Nights, you and I and Winston will stay in this bus— the rest of the guys..." he tossed his head over his shoulder, "will sleep in the other buses. That way we'll get some privacy." He kissed her hand.

Summer smirked. She looked out the window, trying to remain calm. The city quickly fell away behind them, and Summer wasn't sure which made her dizzier, the buzz of the passing landscapes or him. She turned to him, and he smiled. Oh, it was him. Definitely him.

"We don't bother with the jet on short tours like this—more of a hassle than it's worth. And we can certainly stay in a hotel if you'd rather, but I normally stay on the bus because of Winston." He ruffled

Winston's head as he spoke. "Okay by you?" He scratched the slight scruff on his chin and raised his eyebrows.

She nodded, sighing. Malcolm made so many concessions to protect Winston and do what was best for him. She smiled, her whole body feeling warm and happy. Malcolm was simply…amazing. How was it possible she was here? With Malcolm Angel? On his tour bus?

Her thoughts were interrupted by members of the band, who walked up to them, checking in with Malcolm for one reason or another. Each said hello to her, each addressing her by name. Jimmy stopped and kissed her on the cheek, obviously having forgiven her for that horrible night. She flushed, feeling herself turn a bright red.

"Let it go, Sum." Malcolm shook his head, laughing. "Jimmy's not holding a grudge."

She nodded, so lost in his world, she had no ability to plot or plan. All she could do was sit back and enjoy, having no idea what was going to happen next.

****

"I want you to wear this for me…" They were naked in a large sized bed in the back of his tour bus. Soft, puffy blankets were tucked around them, and Winston was asleep at their feet. Malcolm's show had been a huge success in Philadelphia, and they were heading farther south. Malcolm was dangling his St. Francis medallion in front of Summer. She reached up and touched it, tentatively.

"Planning to strip onstage?" She giggled, twirling the medal in his grasp.

"Something like that. This way, if you're wearing

it, sitting in the front row—it'll still be like the medallion is on me. It'll bring me luck."

Summer inhaled deeply. What was happening here?

"Don't wanna?" He raised an eyebrow.

"Of course I do."

"C'mere…"

He pulled her up to sitting, and the blankets fell away from her breasts. He smiled at her, and she didn't bother to cover up.

"You are so beautiful."

She turned her back to him and lifted her hair. He placed the medal around her neck and clasped it. He leaned forward, kissing the back of her neck, softly…over and over…

She raised her shoulders. When the excitement was too much to stand, she let her hair flop down around them. He reached forward and clasped her breasts, holding her, his fingers rolling her nipples. Some of her hair caught in his grasp, tickling her. Immediately, her already taut nipples hardened with his touch. He leaned forward, kissing her ear, gently.

Tiny bumps sprouted up and down her body. She tried to turn to him, but he held her still.

"I want you like I have never wanted another woman. Ever…"

Air expelled from her lungs like water rushing over a waterfall, and she gasped to take a breath. He removed his hands from her breasts, and kissed her shoulders, wrapping his hands around her soft belly. His strong hands, callused from years of playing guitar, made their way to her lap. He reached down between her thighs, separating them, and then his fingers moved back upward, settling.

"God..." He moaned into her ear as his finger explored the length of her.

She was already so wet, her body ached to be with him. She leaned back against him, loving the feel of his incredibly strong arms holding her. His finger settled in just the right spot, and Summer reached up behind her, arching her back, grasping his neck. After a few more minutes of constant pleasure, his finger made its way downward, pushing its way in.

"Oh, Malcolm..." She turned her head demurely, rubbing her cheek against his shoulder—surrendering all control.

Having Malcolm Angel inside her made her wild. She craned her neck, turning back to him, and he kissed her, full on the mouth. His tongue made its way into her mouth as his finger slid in and out. Holding her by her inner thighs, he pulled her up onto his lap. Her breath rushed from her as he slid on a condom. Still with her back to him, he lifted her. Her eyes flew open, and she gasped as he brought her down on top of him.

"Malcolm..."

He pushed harder against her as her legs opened wider, making room for him.

"That's good..." Malcolm purred into her ear. "Summer, baby, that's so good..."

He tucked her legs beneath her, wrapping them around his hips. He lifted and lowered her hips in time with him. He pulled her closer, covering her neck and back with kisses, and reached around, his hands finding her nipples once again.

She cried out. Malcolm grabbed her hair with one hand, pulling her head backward, and with the other, he touched her again until she trembled hard against him. She went limp, and Malcolm leaned her forward, sliding a pillow under her hips. He stayed behind her, his thrusts harder...and stronger...and deeper. He grabbed her hips tightly, and she could feel he was teetering on the edge. He grasped her hair again and pushed into her, completely. She clenched her jaw and moved her hips higher, driving him even deeper—never wanting this to end.

"God, Summer..."

Summer's teeth chattered as he finished. He released his hold on her and sat back on his heels, panting. She wiggled her hips down against the pillow. Her head was turned, her cheek against the mattress, her hair cascading across the pillow.

He slid forward and lay on top of her, kissing her cheek. "Did I hurt you?"

"No. I—I loved it..." She smiled, her arms folded under her pillow.

Carefully, he rolled off of her and onto his back. He pulled her against him, and while the miles of road rolled by beneath them, she fell asleep with her head on Malcolm Angel's chest.

****

Summer sat in the front row, her eyes glued on Malcolm. He moved like a god onstage. He was born to be there, he owned the stage...and when he pointed his mic toward her and threw her a kiss with his two fingers, he owned her, too. The pull between her legs assured her of that.

The medallion she wore around her neck warmed with her flush, and she sat, mesmerized, as Malcolm sang song after song for thousands of screaming fans.

When he sat downstage on his stool, Summer, like everyone, knew he was preparing to sing his most famous love ballad—but only she knew what it meant.

"Hey, there…" Malcolm crooned into the microphone. He sat with one leg on a rung on the stool, the guitar across his lap. He was so, so…sexy.

Summer shivered, feeling the bumps up and down her arms, knowing what was waiting for her only hours from now. She pushed her thighs against the seat, forcing herself to stay still. She wanted him—so much. Now. She'd wait only as long as she had to. Tonight, as he showered off his performance, she would join him. She smirked at her plan, and he smiled at her from stage.

"Well," Malcolm ran his hand up through his hair.

The audience went wild in response.

"As most of you know—"

"We love you, Malcolm!"

"I love you, too, guys." He lifted his arm, pointing to the seats in the upper levels. And then his eyes made their way to Summer.

"Huh…" Her breath hitched, and she sat back in her seat, trying to keep from hyperventilating.

It was barely perceptible, and it lasted for only a micro-moment, but Malcolm Angel absolutely looked at her when he said, "I love you."

Summer's eyes widened, and she looked immediately at the floor. She had to let him off the hook. It was all chance, for certain. The world's most confirmed bachelor was not telling her he loved her. It was impossible. Besides, romantic love didn't exist. She knew this. It was a money making ploy created by card companies. Successful couples built relationships on mutual respect and similar goals....that was all. She took a deep breath and looked back up at the stage.

He smiled, laughing to himself. "So...you know what's comin'...and I know what's comin'...so whaddaya say we break the rules tonight?"

The audience applauded wildly.

"Whaddaya say we're a little...bad..." He said the word with his mouth tight to the microphone, and Summer's heart raced in response. Good grief how she wanted him—inside her—right now.

"We love you!"

This time Malcolm just lifted his arm in response, and his drummer began a slow beat Summer didn't recognize.

"You guys..." Malcolm smiled and turned back to Jimmy, saying something no one else could hear. Jimmy nodded in response. Malcolm turned back to the audience. "You guys are special."

Thunderous applause rocked the arena.

"Yeah, I knew you were special."

Jimmy joined in now, also with a slow, sexy rhythm, new to Summer.

"I'm gonna play something for you. And only for you."

The audience screamed and cheered, people jumping up and down on their seats.

"Well, because it's summer. And summer's my favvvorite..." he dragged the word out, "...season. How 'bout you?"

Summer's breath quickened. Was it just a coincidence he was singing a song about summer...now? Why hadn't he ever written one before he met her? She covered her ears, the earplugs offering little buffer from the screaming crowd.

"Then," the slow sexy beat kept up, "after I play somethin' new—I'm gonna play you somethin' old."

His eyelids were heavy, and her body responded to him with a familiar ache. She took a deep breath and pushed it out her mouth.

"This way…we do it twice. Whaddaya say?"

The audience screamed in response, and Malcolm looked deliberately at Summer. She grinned.

"So I'm just gonna give you a little tease here…but we all like a little foreplay, right?"

Screams shook the arena, and security stopped three different women from trying to grab Malcolm onstage.

Malcolm didn't even notice the mayhem, instead his face adopted a look of stern concentration, and he began strumming his guitar. The band joined in as he sang.

"People often ask me, and what can I say? The warmest sun on me on the coldest winter day…"

He shook his head, playing along.

"Nah, not for me—I'm forever wild and free. No choice I'll make, no other I'll forsake…"

Summer swallowed hard.

"Sometimes people wonder, is it the sound of the thunder…echoing tonight, bringing charge to my respite…"

"Nah, not me…no one I can see. I take 'em all the same, the pieces in my game."

Summer's jaw clenched.

"I've been asked before, is there one at your door? Who'll silently await, touched by the hand of fate…?"

"Nah, not me…I'm lost in my own sea…no land in

sight, no hand to hold tight…"

"And then Summer… Mmm-mm, hmmm… And then, Summer…Mmm-mm, hmmm…"

"You see: I'm no good at all, my heart's an empty ball…beating recklessly…tiring effortlessly…"

"And then Summer… Mmm-mm, hmmm… And then, Summer…Mmm-mm, hmmm…"

"Your eyes the color of the sincerest night…your voice gave purpose to my flight…"

"And then Summer… Mmm-mm, hmmm… And then, Summer…Mmm-mm, hmmm…"

"Because of all the men I can choose to be, I'd be the one you'd want from me…I've walked on fire and cried in rain, felt so dead there was no pain. You gave me hope and nursed my scar, saved me from myself so far…so yeah, it's Summer…"

"Mmm-mm, hmmm… It's Summer…Mmm-mm, hmmm…"

"Summer. The only place I want to be, because Summer…you're every single season… to me."

He finished the song, letting his head drop. As the crowd went wild with applause and cheers, Summer reached up to wipe a tear from her eye. He turned to her and smiled. She inhaled, smiling back.

Chapter Seventeen

Sitting on the tour bus, Summer leaned her head against the window, enjoying the beautiful scenic country whizzing by. Malcolm sat next to her, working out new songs, his guitar on his lap. She petted Winston, smiling, knowing this was as close to heaven as she had ever been. She loved the old farms with the giant red barns and tall silos. She breathed deeply, imagining the sweet smell of grass in the country air. She inhaled Malcolm, and closed her eyes as she fantasized about the two of them, on just such a farm, together. How absurd.

Her head rolled back toward Malcolm. He was writing and rewriting a piece of music—humming something, scribbling furiously, and then cursing under his breath as he erased. She snickered; did he know he talked to himself while he worked? Of course he did— his work was writing music. Did he know he furrowed his brow when he concentrated? Or that he scratched the scruff on his chin when he contemplated something new? Did he know the corners of his eyes crinkled when he smiled, or that his eyelids grew heavy when he made love to her? Summer shifted in her seat and glanced around a full tour bus, suddenly wishing it was only the two of them.

It wouldn't matter now anyway, because Malcolm was working. He worked a lot, and incredibly hard. She shook her head thinking of the millions of people who believed being a rock star was easy. And why shouldn't they? Malcolm made it seem that way. He never let them see the hours of rehearsal and practice, the endless nights of writing and rewriting, the commitment to staying in top physical shape. He was an artist, athlete, and lover, all rolled into one. And thankfully, at this moment, he was her lover. She snuggled into herself, happier than she ever dreamed possible.

They hadn't spoken most of last night. He was quiet when he came offstage. He simply took her hand and led her back to the tour bus. They made love, passionately, hungrily, with Malcolm on top of her, his eyes locked on hers. Millions of words were thought between them, but for the longest time, neither of them was brave enough to utter a single one.

When he finished, Malcolm lay on top of her. Finally, he spoke.

"Sometimes I'm so tired, I'm grateful I'm getting older—just so I'm that much closer to the finish line."

She wrapped her arms around him and held him tightly. She whispered, softly. "That is the saddest thing I have ever heard."

He pushed himself up, resting on his elbows, his fingers tracing her cheeks, gently.

"But now…now I'm not in such a rush anymore."

He kissed her completely.

On the bus, Summer ran her fingers across her lips absentmindedly, thinking of his kiss. She adjusted her white and yellow peasant blouse, the one she had worn on their first date. Her movement caught Malcolm's attention.

"That's still my favorite shirt." He grinned. "The

only thing I like more is when you're wearing my t-shirts. Or, uh, even better, no shirt at all..." He leaned over and kissed her, like they were a married couple, celebrating an anniversary.

She giggled.

Malcolm gazed past her and out the window, his attention drawn outside. "Why're we slowing down?"

The bus came to a stop. The driver popped his head back into the seating area to talk to Malcolm.

"Sorry, Malcolm. Construction. In the middle of the country. Who knew?" He threw up his hands and disappeared back to the cab of the bus.

Malcolm snickered, and Summer noticed several of his band members gathering on the opposite side of the bus, staring out a window.

"Something's got their attention." Summer pointed to the window, and Malcolm turned to see.

"What're you guys looking at?"

Malcolm's drummer, Eric, turned to him. "A cow. Doing some weird dance thing. Stepping side to side, then lifting her tail and trying to squat. Looks like the farmer's dancing with her. Maybe he's going to put it up online. Pretty amusing."

Summer sat up straight. "What? What cow?" She slid Winston off her lap and made her way to the window, where she saw a malnourished cow with a swollen belly, moving exactly as the drummer described. Summer swiveled her head back and forth, her eyes searching the field, desperately looking for some sort of assistance for the cow, but the old farmer was all alone.

"Darn it." Summer turned back.

The bus began to roll forward, slowly.

"Malcolm, stop the bus."

"What?" Malcolm shook his head. "What are you talking—"

"Please, Malcolm. Make him pull over. Stop the bus." Summer pushed past Malcolm and ran to the bathroom. She scrubbed her hands, making them as sterile as possible. She emerged just as the bus was slowing down. She kept her hands elevated, her elbows bent.

"Summer, what's going on?" Malcolm narrowed his brow, reaching for her.

Summer turned away. "You can't touch my hands right now. I'm sterile. Or as close as I can get. That cow needs help." The members of the band were staring at her. "I need someone—maybe more than one of you—who can stand blood and a lot of it. Follow me."

Summer dashed down the steps and, as best she could, hoisted herself over the highway guardrail without using her hands. She ran across the pasture with Malcolm on her heels.

The farmer looked up at her.

"I'm Dr. Wynters, DVM. I'm a veterinary surgeon." She caught her breath.

"Thank God, my cow...what's wrong?" The farmer was as old as a great-grandfather, with a kind, sad face.

Malcolm looked at her, shaking his head. He narrowed his eyes, completely confused. "What are you talking about? You're a doctor? A—a surgeon?"

"Yes." Summer sighed. "I'm sorry, Malcolm. Really. Please, please, I'll explain everything as soon as I can. Right now—"

The cow let out a moan of agony. Summer hushed

the cow, her eyes gazing over the cow's beautiful rich brown color and white face.

"Please, Malcolm. Just let me do this and give me a chance."

Malcolm stepped back.

Summer turned to the farmer. "What's your name, Mr.…?"

"Randolph." He wheezed when he spoke, exposing brown teeth. "Jeb Randolph."

"Okay, Mr. Randolph. Your cow is suffering from dystocia. She won't be able to give birth on her own. How long has your cow been in labor?"

"I'm not sure."

Summer breathed deeply. "Okay. We need to get the calves delivered soon."

"There's more than one?"

Wishing, in vain, for latex gloves, Summer palpated the cow's abdomen. "Judging from the size of her belly, I'm guessing twins. They're often a problem."

Summer walked behind the cow, and the cow twitched, mooing in agony.

"Has she dropped her water sac yet?"

The farmer pushed up his hat and scratched his head, moving much slower than Summer needed him to. "Hard to say…"

"Did anything come out of her yet? Round? Like a…a balloon filled with water?"

"Oh yeah…saw something like that. She dropped it up closer to the farm."

Summer nodded, knowing her window of opportunity was quickly closing. Waiting too long to assist a cow in stage two of the birthing process can mean death for the calf and cow. "We need to proceed now. How far is your farm?" Summer looked over the land, surveying the situation. "I need to get her into a chute and headgate."

"At least two miles that way." He pointed behind them.

Summer dropped her head, thinking. She turned to Jimmy and a few other men who followed her out. "You'll need to hold her. And I need..." Summer wracked her brain, never having delivered calves in an open pasture with no equipment. Darn it, why couldn't she be in a fully stocked operating room? Or at least in a barn? "I need rope. Do you have some on the bus?" She looked at Malcolm.

"Probably." He nodded.

"I might. I definitely have bungee cords for the percussion instruments." Eric was up and gone before she could answer.

Summer spoke calmly to Jimmy. "When he gets back, I'll rope her. If we're lucky, she'll drop before parturition."

"What?" Jimmy shook his head.

"Birthing. It will help us if she's down." Summer spotted Eric heading into one of the back tour buses. "The most important thing is not to allow her to kick back. She'll fight me as I reposition the calves. My guess is the fetal position is wrong—possibly breech." Summer thought long and hard, breathing deeply.

The cow began to drop.

"Get back," Summer put up her arms, pushing the men away from the cow. "She's ready." Summer nodded to the farmer. "This position will help."

Eric ran back with the bungees, throwing them to

Summer.

Quickly, Summer roped the cow's forelegs and pulled them, handing the bungee to Eric. "Hold it as tightly as you can."

He nodded, his eyes wide.

"You sure about this, Summer?" It was Jimmy.

"Absolutely not. I work in operating rooms, not in fields. But I'm certain she needs help." Summer squatted down again, palpating the abdomen.

The cow panted heavily.

Summer looked up at the members of the band, staring at her. "If you're squeamish at all—leave now."

Eric dropped the bungee, stuffing his hands in his pockets. He shuffled his feet. Jimmy picked it up.

"In two minutes I am going to put my hands into this cow, reposition the calves, and then pull them out. There will be mucus, placenta, fluids, and more blood and gore than in a horror movie. I won't have time to help you if you pass out."

Eric nodded and stepped backward, quickly. He turned and broke into a sprint, heading back to the bus.

"Okay." Summer turned to Jimmy. "How many kids do you have?"

"Uh…three."

"Were you in the delivery room?"

He nodded. "One natural, two C-sections."

"Perfect, come here next to me."

Malcolm took the front cords Jimmy had dropped. Summer's eyes darted up to Malcolm, wondering if all this blood was going to trigger a memory. She shook her head. She needed to focus on the cow—not on Malcolm.

Summer tied the hind legs and handed the cords to

Jimmy. "Pull the legs here, when she resists, pull tightly."

Summer swallowed hard, her eyes making their way back to Malcolm. His eyes locked on hers. She exhaled. Out of the corner of her eye, she saw the farmer scratch his head again, and pet his cow, gingerly. She bit her lip, focusing on the task at hand.

"Mr. Randolph, you have a malnourished Hereford in dystocia. My guess is twins. She's already dropped the water sac, and there's no significant progress. If she doesn't birth within two hours of the drop—she will die. Your cow is in distress. Do I have your permission to assist her? You understand although I am a board-certified veterinary surgeon, there is a risk to any assistance, and your cow and calves may perish. I am not sterile, and I may bring infection to the cow or calves, which may cause complications for further pregnancies. Do you want me to proceed?"

"Yes, yes...please." The farmer kept petting his cow.

"Okay." Summer took a deep breath and squatted down beside the cow. Slowly, she inserted her hands into the birthing canal. "Darn it." She shook her head. She looked up at Malcolm as if he could understand her, her arms elbow deep inside the birth canal of a cow. "I've got the tail."

"What does that mean?" Jimmy was doing a good job at remaining upright.

"Means we're out of time."

Summer glanced up and saw Malcolm studying the farmer. He understood the farmer's worries.

"I have to bring the hind legs up, and then we'll have to move incredibly fast."

Perspiration dripped off Summer's forehead, itching her, but there was no way she could scratch it.

"I need another bungee."

Within a flash Malcolm was at her side.

"You may not want to be here…it's not pretty."

Malcolm didn't budge.

"Okay." She nodded, looking up at the farmer. "Mr. Randolph, I'm going to push the first calf farther into the uterus. Once I get the legs into the birthing canal, I'm going to tie a cord on, and I'm going to start pulling. This calf will be born breech, so you have to prepare yourself for the worst."

The farmer removed his hat and squatted down next to the cow, rubbing her back.

Summer exhaled, forcefully. "Mr. Randolph, grab her tail, and hold it upright for me. It will help me with the repositioning."

The farmer did as she asked.

Summer took another deep breath and managed to reposition the calves hind legs into the birthing canal. Malcolm handed her the cord, and she quickly tied a double-half hitch knot on the legs.

"Here goes…"

She inhaled deeply and sat back, beginning to pull. She tugged gently at first, gauging her success rate. Not nearly enough. She needed way more strength. Summer stood now, digging her feet into the earth. She pulled out and down, harder, and the calf began to move, but again, not nearly enough. The cow mooed in agony.

"He's fighting me…" Summer spoke through clenched teeth. "The cow needs a c-section, but the barn's two miles away, and I have no equipment. So we're going to have to do it this way." She clenched her teeth and bore down again. She wasn't pulling fast enough or hard enough. She just did not have the physical strength to do it. "Darn it." Summer shook her head, adrenaline coursing through her. Maybe it would give her the boost she needed.

"Tell me what to do." Malcolm took the blood stained cords from her hands.

She gaped at him, breathing heavily.

"I need you to pull back and down." She saw Malcolm's muscles flex in his t-shirt—he was incredibly strong. Maybe too strong. "The knot I tied should protect the calf's legs, but you'll have to be careful. Too much force and we'll injure the calf. I'll guide the cord…just match my movements."

Malcolm's eyes locked on her. He nodded and moved behind her, holding the cord with her.

"Ready…"

She began pulling, and Malcolm did the same.

"We need to move quicker—a little more force..."

Malcolm increased his pressure, and the calf moved quickly.

"Hold on." Summer inserted her hands, checking the position of the calf. He was as well positioned as possible. She grabbed the cord again. "Okay, one more pull…" her voice strained as she and Malcolm successfully pulled the calf from its mother.

"Fuck." Malcolm squatted down behind her.

She exhaled, audibly, and suppressed a giggle. Immediately, she went to work on the calf.

"Come on…" Summer spoke under her breath as she cleaned out the calf's nose with her fingers, tickling its nose to get the calf to breathe. She repeated her actions.

"How long…?" Malcolm was standing next to her.

"We've got sixty seconds, that's all. Come on…darn it." She repeated the actions once more, cleaning the nose. This time she grabbed a blade of grass and tickled the nose.

There it was. The tiniest flicker of the nostril.

"Summer…" Malcolm pointed to the nose. "Did you see that?"

She nodded, exhaling. Her shoulders relaxed. "Okay. Mr. Randolph, the calf is alive. We need to move her away and birth the other."

With Malcolm's help, they untied the bungees, and moved the calf to an open space. She turned back to see Malcolm was nearly as stained in blood as she was.

She fought the urge to put her arm on him, making sure he was okay. She wondered if the blood was too much for him.

She shook her head, forcing herself back to work on the cow. Thankfully, the second calf delivered much more easily.

****

Once both calves were nursing, and Summer had delivered the placenta, she sat back on the grass, her arms covered in blood. She rubbed her shoulder against an ear to scratch an itch.

Using her cell, the farmer placed a call, and his grandson was on his way from town with a flatbed truck lined with straw to transport the cow and her calves.

"Thank you, Dr. Wynters." Mr. Randolph held out his hand.

Summer wiped the blood from her hands onto the grass, but they were still stained a deep crimson.

Nevertheless, she stood and shook the farmer's hand.

He clutched her bloody hand with both of his. "Thank you, thank you."

Summer stared at the man's toothless grin and worn boots. He was struggling, from his head to his toes. She sighed, smiling at him.

"I'm just happy it all worked out."

"Yes, yes." The farmer beamed at her, finally letting go of her hand. "But Doctor, I know you must be expensive…what with how smart you are and all."

Summer scoffed and caught Malcolm's slight grin.

"But money's a bit tight." The farmer lifted his hat, exposing very fine thinning hair, and then replaced it. "I'll find a way, but it may take some time…"

"Mr. Randolph, I don't want your money. But what I do want is for your cows to eat better. This Hereford is malnourished." Summer used a stern tone when she spoke, pointing at the cow. "I know money can be tight, Mr. Randolph, but your cows have to eat better. There are subsidies for farmers such as yourself. The government can assist you. Do you understand?"

"Yes. But how?"

Just then the grandson pulled up in his truck. Malcolm hung back, making sure he wouldn't be recognized, as Summer took a few minutes to explain the options to the grandson.

After she finished lecturing the farmers, and both men promised to take better care of the cows, Summer smiled sweetly.

The grandson made his way back behind the wheel—his distance and preoccupation assuring Malcolm's continued anonymity.

Just as the farmer was about to climb into the cab

of his truck, he turned back. "A young doctor like you…helping an old man like me. Thank you. And so beautiful, too." He tipped his hat when he spoke. "I'm sure you're taken, but if not, my grandson is quite a fine young gentleman."

Summer snickered at the groan coming from inside the truck.

"It was my pleasure. And thank you for the compliment, Mr. Randolph."

The farmer snapped his jaw shut, giving up. He climbed into the truck with a final, "Thank you, Dr. Wynters, thank you."

Mr. Randolph was still smiling as the truck pulled away.

Malcolm was not.

Chapter Eighteen

Malcolm continued to stare at her. How? How could he have been so wrong? He studied her with her soft, white peasant shirt doused in red…the color of betrayal. She looked like a fallen angel.

All around, the ground was covered in blood and guts—another accident scene—another end to something wonderful.

How fitting. Here it was, the second time his life was ending, and it was exploding with all the spectacle of another horrible accident. He was dying for a second time, and he deserved it. Because this time the accident was intangible—this time, the disaster came from trusting her.

"Malcolm…" Her voice was soft, her eyes welling with tears. She took a step toward him.

He put up his hand and shook his head.

She nodded, looking down at the ground.

Jimmy spoke. "Hey, uh, I'm going to go check on the buses…and the guys." He walked off, leaving them alone.

Malcolm shook his head, tears threatening his eyes. "All I wanna know is, why? Why didn't you tell me?"

"I—I wanted to."

Summer stepped closer, and Malcolm ran his bloody hand through his hair. He wanted to hold her—more than anything—but this gnawing ache in his gut would not allow it. How? Why? Why would she lie? After everything? After what they had shared? And who the hell did he think he was to be happy? This was fitting. He deserved to be betrayed. There was no room in his life for love. He breathed heavily, keeping his anger in check.

"Malcolm, please, believe me."

"Believe you?" His eyes danced with fury. "Why should I believe anything you say?"

She swallowed hard as tears streamed down her cheeks. "I know I deserve that. But please let me try to explain. Jeanette told me—"

"Wait." Malcolm held up his hand again. "Was this all a set up?" He heard the vulnerability in his voice, wondering how he could be so gullible.

"The first night, only. I went to your concert with Jeanette, hoping you'd notice me."

"For what? To get your kicks with a…a rock star before you settle down to some nice suburban life with a good-guy doctor husband?"

"No." She shook her head, forcefully. "No. I had the chance for all of that, but it's not what I want."

Malcolm stepped backward, a stab of jealousy hitting him square in the heart. So the other man, he had wanted her all for himself, too. Malcolm ground his teeth, fighting the urge to sweep her up and make her his—for good.

Her eyes pleaded with him, begging for understanding. "Yes, I have one summer. Yes, I wanted to be with you before I really knew you. But now that I know you, I want to be with you even more. And yes, it was horrible, and I never should have lied about being a model, but Jeanette said you would only…be with…models…so I lied, hoping you'd find me more attractive."

Malcolm began to see red. "Yeah, well, let me tell you—I never, not once, believed you were a model." He set his jaw.

She nodded, biting her lip. She looked down at the ground.

Crap. He didn't mean it. Not like that, anyway. She was the most stunningly beautiful woman he'd ever known. He loved her body more than the bodies of all the swimsuit models he'd slept with. Watching Summer's shoulders slump and her face redden, he felt terrible—like a horrible bully. But he was just so angry…

To her credit, she faced him and smiled a small smile. "I know that. You're a smart man. I'm sorry I lied. And I'm sorry I perpetuated the lie. I didn't think being a vet would be sexy enough for you, I guess."

Malcolm shook his head, couldn't she understand her brain and capabilities were two of the things he liked most about her? That what she just did—how she saved the cow and the calves and even that farmer—how that was so much sexier than a woman who simply poses on the cover of a magazine?

"I was afraid if I told you the truth, it would ruin everything. Instead, I ruined everything by keeping quiet."

"You didn't ruin everything."

Summer raised her eyes to him. Her entire face was gorgeous—soft and feminine—but those eyes… Time and again he had found himself lost in those eyes. Hope flashed in her smile, and she inhaled deeply. Malcolm's chest was heaving.

"You didn't ruin everything, because there was never anything to ruin."

"Oh." She swallowed hard and stepped back. "I—I'm sorry."

They stood for minutes more, with Malcolm's eyes fixed on her, memorizing every detail of the soft, beautiful person she was. He wished he could change everything he just said. But it wouldn't matter. He had no right to be happy, and the sooner he let her go, the better. His hands balled into fists, which he clenched and released, repeatedly.

Jimmy approached cautiously. Neither Malcolm, nor Summer, turned to him.

Jimmy cleared his throat. "Hey, guys, what do you say we hit the road? We have a long trip ahead."

The sunlight bounced off Summer's hair, and the acrid feel of betrayal burned through Malcolm's veins.

"No." Malcolm shook his head. He still had a few stops left on the tour. How dare she weaken him like this? "No."

Malcolm stepped forward, facing Summer. He swallowed, hard. Ire rose inside him like a fast moving fire. He knew, once again, he was about to destroy everything in his wake, but he couldn't help himself.

"Jimmy," Malcolm's eyes were locked on Summer as he spoke, "take Dr. Wynters to one of the accessory buses. Let her get cleaned up. Then have someone escort her to the nearest airport. Make sure she has enough money for her flight, and all expenses."

Summer's chest heaved uncontrollably.

"Mal," Jimmy's voice was quiet and brotherly. "Are you sure—?"

Malcolm just nodded.

Summer began to back away, free flowing tears falling down her cheeks. "Malcolm, this doesn't have to be like this. I made a mistake, yes..."

He turned away, unable to look at her.

She nodded, wiping her cheeks with her bloody hand. "You know what? I think you're happy about this. I think I just made it easy for you. I just gave you the out you needed." She turned and ran for the bus.

Malcolm stared after her as she climbed the steps of one of the buses, remembering the first time he watched her climb the stairs of his tour bus—the beauty of her hair, the softness of her shirt, the roundness to her jeans. She had teased him then, flirting with him, giddy and fun. Surprisingly, a smile swept across Malcolm's face at the memory, and then a radiating pain shot down his arms—identical to the last time he had lost someone he loved. Malcolm shook his head, rubbing the pain in his chest, trying desperately to make it—all of it—disappear.

Summer vanished into the bus with one final gaze over her shoulder, and this time, Malcolm was certain this would be the last time he would ever see her.

****

Summer let herself into her tiny apartment. She sighed, heavily, dropping her bags. It was a nice enough apartment, small, but clean. She had a tiny white kitchen, with an attached dining room that's sole purpose was to house her mother's dining room set and china. She never used that room—ever. In the living area she had a deep blue couch, and a wingback chair. Her desk was situated in front of a window, with a beautiful view of the backyard. Off the living room was her bedroom that contained a white wrought-iron bed frame, a tall dresser, and a small closet. It didn't matter the closet was small, Summer hardly had any clothes. And since she hadn't bothered to go back to New York to get the rest of her things out of Jeanette's apartment, she had even less. But Summer couldn't fathom facing New York or Jeanette. Jeanette could trash Summer's stuff for all Summer cared.

Summer plopped down onto her belly on the couch and buried her face in a cushion. Something tickled her chin.

"Huh," Summer sprung up with a gasp. The medallion. She had forgotten to give it back. What should she do? She couldn't mail it, it was too big a risk. Maybe she'd see him again and could give it to him then? The tears that dropped, big, round, and heavy with memories, told her that would never happen. She clutched the medallion in her hand, holding it to her body. She lay down on her back and gazed at the exposed beams of her tiny cottage apartment. Holding Malcolm's medal in her hand, she drifted off.

****

The days blended into a week. Malcolm's tour would be ending soon. Not that it mattered. He'd probably forgotten about her already; probably already replaced her with six or seven gorgeous women who truly were models. Wedged into the corner of her couch, papers and journals around her, she sighed.

Summer pulled herself from the couch. Burying herself in work, catching up on papers she had been neglecting, none of it made her feel any better. She paused to consider this is exactly what she did when her parents had passed. She stood, stretching, the room suddenly spinning. Darn. She had forgotten to eat, in—

she cocked her head, thinking. When was the last time she had eaten?

She fiddled with the medal around her neck. This wasn't healthy—any of it. She took a deep breath and marched to the kitchen. She pulled open the door of her empty fridge, tears rushing to her eyes when she thought of flirting with Malcolm in his kitchen. She wiped her tears in her t-shirt.

"That's it. This stops now." She spoke the words aloud so she would at least attempt to believe them. She yanked open a cupboard and pulled out a hardly used pot to boil water. She marched to her pantry and grabbed a box of pasta. Again she checked the empty fridge, hoping she would miraculously find a slab of butter. No luck. She slammed the door of the refrigerator, pushing the memory of Malcolm's kitchen out of her head. Why was she still focused on him when he had certainly already forgotten about her?

She checked her cell phone again, sighing. There was no one who was going to call her—no work, no school, no Jeanette…no Malcolm. There was no one, except Dr. Brad. Summer dumped the old, half eaten box of spaghetti into the lukewarm water, not bothering to stir. What did it matter if it came out a gelatinous clump? It's not like she was going to eat it, anyway.

Summer stood there fiddling with her medal, and suddenly some unsolicited advice she had received when her parents passed, sprung to mind. "Don't try to pretend they were never here, instead, allow the wonderful memories you shared guide you toward future happiness." Summer never believed in that advice. She believed squashing pain and focusing on work was the only answer. But now, here, all alone in her tiny kitchen, the thing that kept her going wasn't her work. It was her thoughts of him. Saving the cow and the calves was her life's calling, yes, but having Malcolm there was the only thing that made it memorable.

She put the medal to her lips, and dragged it back and forth across her mouth. So maybe he was gone. But what they had was real—and it would live inside her, as long as she allowed it to.

****

Malcolm stormed offstage. He was pissed. The concert sucked—he didn't care what anyone said. He had forced himself to sing his love song, but his thoughts had continually drifted to Summer. He grabbed a bottle of water and chugged it, finishing it in one gulp. He hurled the empty container across the wing space, watching it bounce off the wall. It landed with an unsatisfying plink. Why? Why did he have to pretend everything was okay? He was so damned sick and tired of pretending. He was so over being him.

"Hey, Mal…"

A beautiful blonde woman in a green dress sauntered past, and all he could think was how Summer wore green the first night he met her. The night that began this whole lie.

The woman stumbled forward, nearly touching him. "Whaddaya say we go back to the bus?"

Where the hell was security? They must have thought she was cool. Well, she wasn't cool—not in any imaginable way. Her breath was hot and reeked of beer. She slurred her words. What kind of woman speaks like that, and throws herself at a man?

Jimmy came running over. "Hey, Mal, why don't I

get you some space…?"

He began to escort the woman away, but Malcolm reached out and grabbed her arm, holding her there. Her arm was cool and slippery. She turned to Malcolm, giggling, her overly made-up face contorting like an ugly clown in a funhouse mirror. Jimmy shook his head.

"Tell me something," Malcolm tossed his head and forced a smile, addressing the woman. "What would you say if after I'm through with you, my friend here has a go of it? He likes my leftovers…"

Malcolm leered, and Jimmy dropped his head.

"K by me," the blonde woman twirled her hair and snapped her gum, sizing up Jimmy. She stumbled as she spoke. "But why wait for you to be done? I'm always up for a party. The more the merrier." She tripped on her high heels.

Malcolm released her arm and shook his head. "Get her outta here…"

Malcolm turned away, disgusted. He walked off to a private area backstage, pacing. He stomped around the equipment that was already beginning to pile up. Most of it belonged to the venue; his equipment was already being loaded onto the buses. This was nearly the last show of the tour—thank God. He was so done. So incredibly done. But now what? Now back to New York to write some more crap about bogus love while he waits for the final show at the Garden—the place he first saw Summer?

"Ugh…" Malcolm grabbed a large amplifier and hurled it clear across the backstage area. This time, the amplifier hit with a satisfying crunch.

Jimmy came running back.

Malcolm put up his hand, without turning in Jimmy's direction. "I'm fine, Jimmy. Fine." Malcolm checked out the damage he'd just caused, his face burning from embarrassment. "Just uh…tell them it was an accident, and make sure it's paid for." Malcolm took a deep breath, turning back, fury draining from his soul. That was it. He was tired of running; tired of shirking responsibility.

Jimmy began to walk off.

"Jimmy, wait." Malcolm stood tall, swallowing hard. "Don't tell them it was an accident. When the press gets hold of my temper tantrum, tell them I threw an object in a confined area making sure no one else would get hurt. I threw it outta frustration, stemming from…personal issues."

Jimmy nodded, his lips curling into a knowing smile. "You got it."

"And Jimmy?" Malcolm raised his eyebrows. "Thanks."

"We've all been there, Mal. Just…just make sure you're not killing the best thing that's ever happened to you."

Malcolm nodded, thinking of Julian and Summer, simultaneously. He ran his hand over his chin. "Of course I am."

Chapter Nineteen

As much as Summer loved work, she hated once again being under the thumb of Dr. Brad. And even more, she despised the idea of heading back to New York—with Brad—for a veterinary convention. She really had no choice. She would meet surgeons at the top of their profession, from all over the world, and she'd learn the latest cutting-edge techniques. She knew if she ever wanted to break out on her own and away from the clutches of Brad, she'd need to make connections. Grudgingly, she agreed to accompany him to the convention. Her only conditions were, one, he understood this in no way meant they were a couple, and two, she had her own hotel room. Truthfully, she wanted to be back in New York—she had been away from the city, and Malcolm, for an entire month.

Summer checked into the hotel the day before the convention began, and that night, she was expected to participate in a dreaded meet and greet, mix and mingle. She hated dressing up for these ridiculous parties. Most of all, she hated all the chitchat small talk she had to endure, while drunken vets twice her age drooled on her cleavage.

Thankfully, that wouldn't be an issue tonight, the dress she was wearing had a high neckline, to cover Malcolm's medallion. She wore that chain always, refusing to take it off—the feel of his medal against her bare skin making him…somehow…closer. Stalling in her hotel room, Summer sat and then stood, sat and then stood, until finally she adopted a sort of squat, hovering over the bed, paralyzed, not knowing what to do next. Her emotions guided her from one extreme to the other: from seething anger, to hysterical tears. Emotions made no sense to Summer, and quite frankly, they threw her for a loop.

Standing upright and pacing back and forth in her hotel room, Summer balled up the sides of her black dress into her sweaty palms. She clumped back and forth in her heels. She wasn't particularly good with people, and these types of social events always reinforced this fact. For the past year or so, she'd always relied on Brad's charm to take over in social situations, but she couldn't do that tonight. Darn it. She stopped moving. Reality bites. Not only would she have to face a roomful of strangers, she would never again face Malcolm.

Sighing heavily, Summer pushed open the door to the bathroom and tore at the zipper of her small makeup bag. Yanking out a brush, she blotted her cheeks with blush and then smeared on some lip gloss. She threw her unbrushed hair into a ponytail over her shoulder. She stared in the mirror—perfectly heinous. Which was exactly how she felt. She didn't want to get dressed up for a party. Frankly, she didn't want to do anything with anyone but him.

She marched into the lounge of the hotel, and Brad turned to her.

"Summer…" His voice was animated, and he held out his hand to her as if they were a couple.

She inhaled deeply, shaking her head. Why was

this so hard? Her legs ached from being in these ridiculous shoes, and her shoulders throbbed as she forced them down, away from her ears. Brad held out a glass of chardonnay, offering it to her. She shook her head and stood there, motionless, staring straight ahead at nothing, until something flickered in the corner of her eye, catching her attention.

Summer turned to a band. The members were dressed in three piece suits, and together, they played annoyingly loud Muzak versions of today's greatest hits. She closed her eyes. Seeing a band, any band, just wasn't okay. Summer turned away from Brad and the music, and glanced around the lounge, her eyes darting from person to person, feeling all eyes on her. What was the problem? Why was everyone staring at her? She rubbed her ears. Why was this horrific music so loud? Changing her mind, she grabbed the wine from Brad and downed it in one guzzle. He raised a judgmental eyebrow in response.

Summer spun around the room, choking on all the suffocating politeness. She put her hand to her neck, and then touched her face, feeling her cheeks warm from the alcohol. Her breathing grew more and more rapid, and she broke out into an icy sweat. She fought to catch her breath, looking around wildly. She backed up until she bumped into the bar. The horrific song ended, and she turned to order herself another wine.

Then, she heard it...the soft chords of the most famous love song in the world. Malcolm's love song. The one he had written for Julian. She swallowed her tears, biting her lip, desperately not wanting to fall apart here...now. She needed to work with many of these surgeons tomorrow. She had to hold it together. And she almost did…until the lead singer began singing.

Summer turned toward the band, covering her ears with her hands. "No, no, no…." she muttered under her breath. How dare he sing Malcolm's song? How could this older, heavyset man with greasy salt and pepper hair think he had the right to sing this song? The song sung by the sexiest, strongest, most talented musician—ever? She reached behind and grabbed the bar, bracing herself, while a wave of possessiveness washed over her, sharp and painful, as if she were doused with an enormous bucket of ice water.

Her knees buckled, and her legs grew wobbly. She fought to stay upright. Malcolm, Malcolm, Malcolm—all she could think was, *Malcolm*. She didn't belong here. She didn't want to be here.

Unfortunately, the only place she truly belonged, the only place she ever really found happiness, is the one place she was no longer welcome.

Summer whipped her head around the room. She raised a shaking hand to her forehead, trying to calm the dizziness. Mercifully, out in the lobby, she spotted the revolving door. With the blemished version of Malcolm's song still assaulting her brain, she let go of the bar and fought her way to the door. She didn't debate telling Brad she was leaving. It just didn't matter anymore. Nothing mattered anymore.

With every bit of strength she could muster, she pushed through the revolving door, and fell out onto the street. She tripped on her shoes, catching herself just before she hit the sidewalk. She threw herself up against the building, sucking in the warm New York air, slowing her pace, trying to keep from hyperventilating. Shapes and cars whizzed by, the street morphing into an animated Christmas tree, with lights and noise and happiness. But there was no happiness for her. Summer put her hand to her mouth, stifling a sob, memories of Malcolm and Winston rushing through her brain.

Her heart ached so completely, she finally understood...nothing is more real than love.

****

"Summer...?" Jeanette wrapped her arms around Summer's neck, yanking her into the apartment. "How? Why?" Her voice was scratchy as she embraced her friend, tightly.

Summer hugged her back, and the two of them stood there, crying in each other's arms. Finally, Jeanette pulled back to take a breath, and Summer's eyes traveled up and down Jeanette's pajamas.

"You're in my pajamas!" Summer laughed, for the first time in over a month.

Jeanette giggled along, and they made their way into the living room.

"I had no idea they were so comfy." Jeanette smiled brightly, and then her face fell. She dropped her chin, and uncontrolled tears began flowing.

Summer hugged her and led her to the couch. Jeanette landed with a plop.

"Wait here..." Summer ran to the guest bedroom and slipped on a pair of her flannel PJs. She grabbed a box of tissues from the bathroom, and then joined Jeanette on the couch. She climbed onto the couch next to Jeanette, wedging the tissues between them.

Jeanette had a bottle of wine going. She leaned forward and grabbed another glass off the coffee table, offering it to Summer.

"No, thanks." Summer shook her head. "I have to work in the morning. I already had one, but it's worn off. I'm afraid I'm going to have to feel every single bit of this."

Jeanette nodded, and Summer grabbed a throw blanket off the chair, spreading it across their laps.

"So…" Summer approached the topic cautiously. "What happened?"

Jeanette clutched her wineglass. "What's to tell? I fell for the wrong guy. Again. I thought…" She stared off, lost in thought, and then turned back to Summer. "I thought he was a nice guy. And…I know it's horrid, but I thought he'd appreciate me, because he doesn't look like the type of guy who normally gets models."

"And?" Summer stroked Jeanette's hair as they spoke.

"And…and it seems I'm not the only model who thought like that. He was seeing three of us—me in New York, another in LA, and a third in Miami."

"Damn." Summer shook her head.

"Yup." Jeanette took a deep breath. "How could I be so stupid? I mean, I know men. I've been around, you know?"

"Jeanette, you can't blame yourself. This was his doing, not yours. You didn't do anything wrong. It just sounds like…"

"What?" Jeanette turned her icy eyes to Summer.

"It sounds like you need to stop looking for the next Superman, and instead, settle for a nice, normal guy." How could she give advice like this when the only man she ever wanted was the antithesis of normal?

"Stop kissing the damned frogs?" Jeanette wiped away a tear.

Summer sighed heavily. Why was giving up on something she never believed in so incredibly hard? "Maybe so."

Jeanette nodded and smiled at Summer. "What about you?"

Summer shrugged. "I'm sure you heard it all."

Jeanette shook her head. "No, actually, that's the strangest part. Malcolm never said a word to anyone. And no one's really seen him since this leg of the tour ended."

Summer narrowed her eyes. She rubbed the spot in her esophagus that burned whenever she was stressed. It was a new symptom that started just about a month ago. Just about the time Malcolm Angel left her for good. "I hope he's okay."

Jeanette reached out and took Summer's hand. "I know you do. Want to tell me?"

Summer nodded. "Everything was great. More than great, actually, it was perfect. Then we were on his tour bus driving through the country, and I saw a cow in distress, so I made Malcolm stop the bus so I could deliver twin calves."

Jeanette stared at Summer with her mouth open. "You what?"

"Oh, yeah. There was blood and gore everywhere. Must have been incredibly sexy to see me with my hands up inside the birthing canal of this poor cow. Oh…" Summer put up her index finger, her voice more energetic. "And let's not forget, for added effect, I was wearing my white peasant blouse that got drenched in blood, and mucus… and afterbirth."

Jeanette burst out laughing, nearly spitting her wine. "I'm sorry, Sum, but I'm trying to imagine the band standing around the middle of a field watching, while you delivered calves." Jeanette laughed harder.

"Great image for their next CD cover, don't you think?" Summer giggled along with her, shaking her head. "It was quite something."

Jeanette turned her entire body to face Summer and smiled, her eyes sparkling. Summer was glad to see Jeanette happy, and glad she was able to share a giggle. Summer had to laugh at the absurdity of it all, because really, there was never a chance for a future together with Malcolm, anyway. Even if Malcolm knew the truth about her from the beginning, it would have to end sometime, right? Malcolm Angel is the world's most confirmed bachelor. And no one, especially not Summer—a plain ol' regular girl, a veterinary surgeon, better with animals than people—would ever change that.

"So," Jeanette prompted her. "What did the guys do?"

"They were surprisingly helpful. I sent the young one, Eric…? You know him?"

"Yeah." Jeanette sipped her wine, enthralled.

"I sent him back to the bus. He looked pretty green. But Jimmy's a dad so he was solid."

"And…Malcolm?" Jeanette approached this carefully, twirling the wine in her glass and speaking through heavy lashes.

"He…he was amazing." Summer smiled. "He stood right by me. And when I didn't have the physical strength to pull the calves from their mother, Malcolm did it for me."

"Wait…" Jeanette sat up on her knees. "Malcolm Angel delivered a calf?"

"Two. And then he figured out I was a vet, and he had a cow." Summer's lips curled into a wry smile.

"Holy crap." Jeanette shook her head, giggling. "Guess people can surprise you, huh?"

"Sometimes." Summer began to slip away, sadness shrouding her. She wiped a tear. "So, uh, Jean, I think I let down womankind. I guess I'm not the one to get away from Malcolm Angel, unscathed."

Jeanette smiled sweetly. "Oh, Sum..." She wrapped her arm around Summer and pulled her near. "I'm so, so sorry."

Summer just nodded and buried her head in Jeanette's shoulder, crying.

****

Summer wore dark glasses on the walk from the hotel to the hospital, hiding her puffy eyes and hangover from crying. It felt so good to be with Jeanette last night, and she was so grateful not to be alone in her hotel...because truthfully, she didn't trust herself. She was terrified she would finally succumb and call Malcolm. All she needed was for him to ask, "Summer, who?" and depression would have rendered her immobile, for sure.

With every step she took, her head pounded from too many repressed memories, aching to be set free. No. She forced her thoughts away and reached up to rub her pounding temples.

"Headache?" Brad looked down at her as they walked.

She shook her head, wanting to pretend Brad wasn't there...and someone else was. But what did she think was going to happen? They would have a happily ever after? She could run a clinic in the middle of the country and tour the world with Malcolm? Not only was this dream incredibly, pathetically naïve, it also wasn't plausible. The time commitment a clinic would demand would be constant; there wouldn't be a spare moment for the luxury of a vacation, never mind running around the world with a rock star boyfriend. And what about this rock star boyfriend? Was he suddenly going to give up his nights with the world's most beautiful women to be with her? Of course not. It was all ludicrous and impractical. She knew better than to be caught up in this schoolgirl silliness.

Summer jammed her shoulders up to her ears, doing her best to ignore Brad's constant jabbering about the horrors of the city. As she gazed around the city lovingly, she didn't agree at all. Sure it had its gritty exterior and rough edges, but underneath it all…underneath…was magic.

Tears pulled across her eyes as sweat began to gather between her breasts. Summer ran the back of her hand across her brow. Could she stand it? Could she handle being in New York without Malcolm, even for one minute more? Every turn, every street, every sound, every smell…reminded her of him. Of course it was completely irrational, but every few minutes she pulled her phone from her pocket and scrolled down…checking…as if she expected Malcolm to magically know she was here. As if he would care… More importantly, where was he? Was he okay? Was Winston?

Pound, pound, pound…Summer moved faster and faster, trying to avoid falling in step with Brad. Brad's arm bumped hers, and she jerked away from him, her eyes narrowing into a hateful glare, a cold shiver tramping down her spine. She shook off her shiver, and felt the ache in her eyes. She didn't want to be here with Brad—he was all wrong: foreign, cold, sterile, and empty. After spending a year and a half with this man, she now hated being with him, and truthfully, maybe she always did.

Summer was so obsessed with her thoughts of Malcolm, she very nearly missed the entrance to the hospital.

"Summer?" Brad held his arm out, showing her the way.

She inhaled sharply and bit her lip. She nodded and walked into the building, with one final glance over her shoulder.

****

In a quiet locker room, Summer changed into blue scrubs that pulled tightly across her chest and pants that hung loosely on her hips. Although she hated to, she slid the medallion off her neck—for the first time since Malcolm had put it there. It was cold and achingly sad without his medal on her, so quickly, she grabbed some surgical tape and taped the medallion to her waist band in the shape of a big "X." That way she would be certain not to lose it. Then she stuffed her bag into a locker. She stood up and breathed deeply, trying to focus on the job ahead, but just then, an irrational fear reached out with its icy, spindly fingers and gripped Summer's heart. She shuddered in response, feeling something…bad…was about to happen. Her heart raced and cold sweat tickled her spine. She knew this feeling. She had felt it twice before...

Malcolm, Malcolm, Malcolm. Again she checked her phone. Nothing. She slipped it into her pocket, with the intent to remove it long before she entered the operating room.

She walked out of the locker room, and Brad held the door for her to enter the prep room. With her hat and face mask secure, Summer entered the prep room to begin the arduous task of scrubbing in.

That's when she felt it. In her pocket—her phone was vibrating. She was certain of it. Without a second thought, Summer rushed from the prep area and into the locker room. She yanked off her hat and mask. Her ponytail fell down her back.

With a shaking hand she pulled her phone from her pocket. "H—hello?"

"Where are you?" Malcolm sounded terrible, exhausted and broken.

"I'm in New York. I just got back last night. You don't sound well, are you okay?" Her heart was beating so fast and loud, she could barely hear his response.

"It's Winston."

Her stomach flipped. She knew this day would come. Brad pushed open the door, following her into the women's locker room.

"Summer, what's going on?"

"Who is that?" Malcolm's voice was stronger.

"No one." Summer turned her back to Brad. "Do you want me to come?"

"Yes." There was no hesitation in Malcolm's voice.

"Summer?" Brad stepped forward.

Summer lifted her finger to quiet him. Her focus was still on Malcolm. "Are you home?"

"Yes."

"I'll be there as fast as I can."

Summer clicked off the phone and grabbed her bag. She pushed past Brad, running out into the street.

****

Luckily, she found a cab right away. She leaned back against the ripped vinyl of the cab seat, her fingers nervously drumming against the window.

"Can you move any faster?"

"Park traffic can be tough." The cabdriver shrugged, throwing up his hands. "You a doctor?" He nodded to her in the rearview. She realized she was still wearing scrubs.

"A vet." Summer sighed, turning the vent of the air conditioning so it blasted against her face. She rubbed her stomach, a horrible ache forming. Whatever was happening in Malcolm's apartment, it wasn't good. Winston was strong, but he was also very, very old.

Summer sat forward, willing the cab to move faster. Time and again she felt the vibration of the phone in her pocket. She checked, but it was only Brad. Needing him to stop, she shot him a quick text. "Sorry I will miss surgery."

"Here ya go." Finally, the cabdriver pulled up in front of Malcolm's building.

Summer stuffed thirty bucks through the partition and raced inside the building. The doorman sent her right up, and security escorted her onto the elevator. No one commented on her scrubs. Maybe it wasn't the first time Malcolm had doctors to his apartment...or...women dressed like nurses. She shook away the ugly thought as the elevator signaled his floor.

She rushed out of the elevator and knocked on Malcolm's door. The door was ajar and pushed open with the slightest pressure. She stepped inside.

Malcolm was sitting on the floor against the wall, with Winston's head resting in his lap. They both appeared exhausted.

"He's barely responsive..." Malcolm's voice was deep, and tired.

Summer nodded, approaching them both tentatively. She squatted down, putting out her hand for Winston to smell it, and he whimpered softly. Summer sat down next to Malcolm and Winston, rubbing Winston's head, gently. Carefully, she pulled back the aging skin of his eyelids, and looked for an answer in his eyes. Unfortunately, it wasn't the answer she wanted, but it was the answer she expected.

She felt under Winston's chin, back behind his ears, and down into his arthritic hips. He whimpered again when she touched him, but his body was immobile. He lay there, panting. Summer sat back, sighing. The last thing this man needed was more bad news.

"Malcolm..." She swallowed hard, pushing herself to remain strong. "There are better, more experienced vets than me. Winston must have an excellent doctor I can call. Or, I have a friend here in the city, a very good surgeon..." Her words faded away.

Malcolm left his head against the wall, but turned slowly toward Summer.

Summer bit her lip, swallowing her sorrow. "He...Winston...you have to know you've both been incredibly lucky. Except for some arthritis, he's been fit and happy. That's why if we call people with more experience than I...they may have answers I don't."

Malcolm shook his head. "There are no answers, Summer. It's over..."

"Yes." She leaned back against the wall, next to Malcolm.

They sat for a few moments, both of them petting Winston.

"Sum?"

"Yes?" Her voice was a whisper.

"I didn't ask you to come as a vet—I asked you to come for me. And for us."

He reached out and took Summer's hand, and she gulped back a sob. Together, they sat in the foyer of Malcolm's penthouse, as Winston passed on their laps.

Chapter Twenty

Malcolm felt it immediately. Even before she did. She could tell, because he squeezed her hand tightly and slid Winston off their laps. He pulled her to her feet, and she looked up at him, confused, crippled by heartache and sorrow.

"Come…" He spoke softly.

"But…" She gazed down at Winston, shaking her head. He looked so alone there, she couldn't bear it. "I have to try something, Malcolm. I—I—it's the only thing I'm good at. Let me try, please…" She pulled away and squatted down beside Winston.

"No, Sum." Malcolm squatted next to her, rubbing her back. "It's not the only thing you're good at. And no one can bring him back. No one. He's eighteen years old. That's—I don't even know. How old is that for us?"

"For a Lab, over one hundred." She swallowed hard, her voice cracking.

"C'mon." He stood, pulling her gently to her feet.

Why was he comforting her? She was the one who needed to be strong for him. She nodded, pushing her tears aside. She took a deep breath, and squared her shoulders, assuming the most businesslike attitude she could muster. "I need to call someone. To…to take the next necessary steps. Are you okay with that?"

"Yes." His eyes were heavy on hers, but he didn't

appear nearly as devastated as she had expected. Maybe he was in shock?

"I can call your vet, I'm sure they'll be discreet." Discreet yes, but it was Sunday and there were so many steps that needed to be taken—steps beyond what a vet's office was prepared to handle—including transporting the body to the crematorium. "Or, I can call the hospital where I was this morning. I have a—a friend there." She looked down at the ground, not wanting to involve Brad. "He might be able to set up a transport for Winston, and we can cut out the middle steps. Although, you probably have a plan set up. Or your vet has options I've never even heard of…?"

"No…" Malcolm smiled. "That's fine. Call the hospital, if you don't mind."

"Okay." Summer nodded and looked down at Winston. She wiped the tears from her eyes and gazed up at Malcolm, simultaneously wanting to protect his privacy and his feelings. "Maybe you should wait on the terrace? So no one knows this is your apartment. Maybe you should just, uh, set it up with your doorman and security so the…uh…transport…comes right up…?" She was stumbling over her words. She hated asking this of him. How could he be so calm?

"Okay. Thanks." Malcolm spoke briefly to his doorman then smiled at her, nodding. He left for the balcony.

Summer took a deep breath and dialed Brad's number.

****

After she hung up the phone, Summer went out to meet Malcolm on the balcony. He was leaning on the railing, looking out over the city. The view was breathtaking.

"Hey…" He spoke without turning to her.

"Hey." She wanted nothing more than to run into his arms, but she had a job to do, and would he want her, anyway?

He turned to her, and her breath hitched. He was so dark and serious and…dangerous… and sexy.

She focused, forcing herself to speak. "The transport will be here in about fifteen minutes. Do you want to say goodbye?"

Malcolm walked up to her and took her hand. Gently, he pulled her back inside. They stood near Winston, and she fell apart. Tears spilled down her cheeks and sobs overtook her breaths. Malcolm reached out with his incredibly strong arm, and pulled her to his chest.

"I—I'm sorry." Her tears flowed freely, drenching his t-shirt.

"For what?" He held her tight.

"For what?" She looked up, her eyes dancing back and forth across his. Her breathing grew faster. Her tight muscles relaxed with his arms, strong and powerful, wrapped around her. She pushed herself closer to him, fearing this would be the very last time she would ever be in the arms of Malcolm Angel. She wept, clutching his t-shirt, wanting nothing more than for him to make love to her, over and over again.

Her jaw clenched and exasperation finally took over. "What am I sorry for?" She pulled back from Malcolm still grasping his t-shirt in her fists—angry at him, angry at Winston, angry at her mother, angry at life, and even angrier at death. "I'm sorry for not being able to help Winston. For not being able to make you feel better…for being upset when he was your dog, and I've only known him a short time."

He grasped her by both shoulders.

She tilted her head, softening with his touch. Her knees went weak, and the only thing keeping her upright was him.

"Summer…" His dark eyes were locked on hers. "Time is not part of the equation of love."

She shook her head, and then nodded, falling against Malcolm. They stayed tight in each other's embrace until the buzzer rang.

"No…" Summer murmured into his chest. "You didn't get to say goodbye."

He shook his head. "I've said too many goodbyes." He looked down at her and smiled, reaching out to stroke her hair.

She nodded, as the tears started again. He let go gently and moved toward the door.

She turned to him. "Malcolm," her words were a hurried whisper. "What are you doing?"

"I'll take care of this. You don't need to." He smiled so sweetly it warmed her heart.

"But this is my job—and you need to stay anonymous."

"I'm through with hiding, Summer. And I'm done with not taking responsibility."

Summer lunged forward and grabbed his hand. "Malcolm," she took a deep breath, a crushing pressure on top of her. "The vet I called to set this up…he was my boyfriend once, but it's been over for a long time."

"I know." Malcolm stroked her cheek. "Dr. Brad Parker. He was your professor, and now, he wants to be your boss."

"Yes." Summer stared, dumbstruck. Her jaw hung open. "How did you know?"

Malcolm smiled and winked at her. She smiled back as he opened the door.

****

"Hi, I'm—Holy Jesus Christ…" The man stepped back when he saw Malcolm Angel at the door.

"I knew I was gonna meet my maker one of these days," Malcolm clasped the man's hand, shaking. "I just didn't expect it to be quite this soon." This had to be Brad—the uneasy feeling in his gut and adrenaline rush told him so.

As he let the man into the apartment, Malcolm turned back to Summer, grinning. Her face was stoic.

"Sorry. Uh…" The man took a second to collect himself. "I'm Dr. Parker. Brad Parker."

Yup. Just as he suspected. Malcolm used the opportunity to size up Brad. Handsome, he never expected anything less. Smart, probably, if Summer dated him. And tall—very, very tall. That, he wasn't expecting. Malcolm took a deep breath, standing up straighter. Come on, Malcolm was six foot one, this guy had to be six-five. That means Summer probably only came up to his abdomen…which meant…oh, hell no. Malcolm's fists clenched, and he began to perspire. The thought of Summer with this man—the thought of Summer with *any* other man… Jealousy spiked Malcolm's blood pressure; he could feel the pounding in his temples. He eyed Brad's suit and shiny shoes, and his tense shoulder muscles released a bit. Nah…not at all right for Summer. She was too grounded and real for a guy in designer suits and spit polished shoes. Malcolm exhaled, regaining control. He smirked, liking the fact his mere presence had thrown Brad off his game, and Brad still hadn't collected himself.

Summer stepped forward, oblivious to the pissing contest Malcolm was clearly winning.

"Brad…" Her voice was stern. She spoke while two men wrapped Winston's body for transport. She pried her gaze away from Winston and forced it onto Brad. "Why are you here? I asked for transport."

Brad shook his head, focusing on Summer. "You said you needed help."

"No. I said I needed transport. And I told you why." She crossed her arms in front of her chest, fuming.

"I thought there was something I could do."

Brad's voice was so smooth and slick, it gave Malcolm the creeps. He shook it off. Summer inhaled deeply as they began to transport Winston. She turned to Malcolm, her voice much sweeter.

"Are you okay if they begin the process?"

He nodded, smiling at her. Brad looked from Summer to Malcolm and back again.

"Ohhh…" Brad raised his eyebrows.

Summer was stern when she spoke to Brad. "What you thought was I needed your help, because I'm incompetent."

"Summer…" Brad laughed in the most condescending way. "I would never have hired you if I thought you were incompetent. You're just inexperienced." He scratched his perfectly shaven chin.

The door closed behind the two transport men, and Winston was gone.

Summer swallowed hard. "I don't need your help, Brad. And I never have. Please stop trying to undermine my confidence."

Brad stood up taller, and Malcolm saw something flash in his eyes. Something he didn't like in the least.

"You never did explain to me how you know Malcolm Angel…? Is that what you did this summer? Play roadie to his show?" Brad's voice was laden with contempt.

Malcolm ran his hand through his hair, breathing deeply, checking his anger.

"He—he's my friend." Summer's voice was soft.

Brad laughed, showing fake white teeth. "Men like this don't have friends Summer, they have conquests." He shook his head. "You're a little girl from the country. You're something he's trying on. When he's done with you, he'll move on to some other Halloween costume profession. You're nothing but a joke to him."

"Hey—"

Malcolm stepped forward and with one hand, pushed Brad up against the wall. Brad landed with a thud. Malcolm pinned Brad with his elbow.

He stared into Brad's eyes. "Like being a bully? Huh?" Malcolm pushed harder against Brad, and Brad squirmed like a roach under his shoe. "I don't care who you think you are, but you're not speaking to her like that. Apologize."

Malcolm dropped his arm and Brad stood up, smoothing his suit, then bam! Malcolm slammed Brad against the wall, pinning him again. Malcolm breathed deeply, not allowing his anger to take control. He narrowed his eyes at Brad. Brad was tall, but he had no strength at all, and Malcolm could see the fear in Brad's eyes.

He was crap. Pure and simple. And he didn't

deserve an ounce of respect from Malcolm. Maybe he was a good doctor, but no man worth his weight would ever speak to a woman like that. Malcolm closed his eyes. Damn. Yes, he had been hurtful too. Those things he said to Summer, they haunted him daily, and he owed her a huge apology. He would explain everything when they were alone—as soon as they were alone— but right now, he was glad this was happening in front of him. Malcolm's shoulders tightened. There was no way he wanted Summer alone with this guy, ever again. He stepped back, dropping his arm. Brad stumbled forward, off the wall. Summer gasped.

"Apologize." Malcolm stood before Brad, his chest heaving.

Brad nodded. "Fine. I'm sorry, Summer. But what are you doing here? The man's an animal. You think he's going to be nice to you?"

"He is nice to me." Summer's voice was strong and solid.

"Then what do you think is happening? You think you're in some sort of relationship with a…a rock star?" Brad laughed, pulling on the lapel of his jacket.

Summer raised her eyebrows.

"Oh, Summer. Don't tell me you fell for this?" Brad pointed to Malcolm. "I thought you were smart, but you're acting like some naïve little teenager. What, you think you're in love?"

Summer's chest rose up and down quickly. She gnawed her lip, working incredibly hard to keep her feelings in check. Malcolm searched her face for the answer. Did she have real feelings for him? She purposely turned away. So there was something she didn't want him to know—but what?

215

Brad took a step toward Summer. "Let me tell you a little something about love, Summer. It doesn't exist. And it certainly doesn't exist with him. He'll use you and toss you aside. And then what do you have? Nothing. You're acting irresponsibly. You have massive amounts of student loans to pay back, unless those elusive parents of yours are actually millionaires."

Malcolm whipped around to face Summer. "He doesn't know?"

Summer shook her head, fear overtaking her eyes. So it was a secret. Her secret. Their secret.

"What don't I know?" Brad dusted the sleeves of his jacket, his voice snide. "Summer? What don't I know?"

"You don't know anything, Brad." She turned away.

"I know one thing." Brad's voice grew louder. "I own you. He doesn't. You can play around with Malcolm Angel all you want, but come Labor Day, you're mine. You've got nowhere else to go. I'll make sure of it." His eyes danced to the beat of some sick power trip. "That little fantasy you have of opening a clinic for large animals and helping farmers in need…what a joke, Summer. How are those poor farmers going to pay you back? In hay? Or apple pie? Do you have any idea what something like that costs? Of course you don't, because you're incredibly foolish about these things. So let me give you your first life lesson. You signed an employment contract—you owe me the next five years of your life. And you're going to regret every single day of it."

"All right. That's it. Get the fuck outta here."

Malcolm stepped forward, and Brad stepped

backward, stumbling. Brad's arms flailed as he tried to steady himself. Malcolm's chest heaved with anger as he stood toe to toe with Brad. Brad's eyes darted like a trapped animal. They landed on Summer. She yanked open the door.

"Summer...this is your choice." Brad backed up toward the opened door. "Come with me now, and I'll choose to forget you spent the summer as Malcolm Angel's whore—"

"You bastard—" Malcolm shoved Brad into the hallway. "The only reason I'm letting you walk outta here is because she's here. But if I ever find out you've contacted her, ever again, you won't be so lucky."

Brad sneered at Malcolm. "Oh, I'll be contacting her. Because come Tuesday, she's no longer yours. She's all mine." He smiled. "Again."

Malcolm slammed the door on Brad.

Chapter Twenty-One

Malcolm leaned with his hand against the door. He looked down at the ground. How had things gotten this crazy? He turned and caught a glimpse of Summer. She was frozen, her eyes locked on his. She looked—terrified.

Malcolm stood up straight, anger coursing through him. Fear was never something he wanted to see in her eyes. "Did he? Has he ever hurt you?" Malcolm pointed to the door with his thumb.

Summer looked at the door and then to Malcolm. "Brad?" She shook her head. "Has Brad ever hurt me?"

"Yeah." Malcolm ground his teeth as he waited for her answer.

She laughed, and Malcolm exhaled.

"Good grief, no, Malcolm." She smiled. "Thank you for worrying." She cast her eyes to the ground. "He's never raised his voice before, unless we're in surgery. Then he yells at everyone." She shrugged. "But we're all used to it."

Malcolm nodded. "Men on power trips—you have to be careful, Summer." His hands balled into fists. He hated the idea of anything happening to her that was out of his control. He didn't want her to have to be careful, or to worry about anything, ever again.

She smiled, and then suddenly, her face grew very, very sad. "Malcolm…"

She chewed her lip—that poor defenseless lip. He wanted to kiss it gently, over and over again.

"Yeah?"

"I—I'm sorry. For all of this. I'm incredibly sorry the last moments of Winston's life were tinged with…this…" She threw up her hands in despair.

Malcolm stepped forward. "Hey…"

She looked up at him, and he smiled. God she was beautiful, and smart, and his body ached to pull her near.

He reached out and tucked a hair behind her ear. "The last moments of Winston's life were with us. Just the two of us."

"Malcolm…?"

"Yeah?"

"How come you're not…more upset about Winston? I'm not judging, I'm just trying to understand."

He leaned his forehead against hers, breathing her in, deeply. "Because he was never really mine. I was just taking care of him for awhile. Now, he's finally where he belongs."

Summer pulled back, understanding. "He was Julian's dog."

"Yes." Malcolm nodded, smiling at her. "And finally, after all this time, they're together."

"Is that what you were staring at on the balcony before…?"

Tears flooded her eyes, and he wiped a single drop that slipped down her cheek.

"Making sure they're both doing fine."

She reached up and stroked his face. Her touch was warm and filled with promise. He placed his hand over hers, holding it tightly to his cheek.

"Wanna know something?"

"Hm?" She closed her eyes.

He took her hand from his cheek, kissing her palm. She opened her eyes.

"There was this book I used to read to…Julian…" Malcolm swallowed hard. "He was much too young to understand it, but it was a beautiful book about a tree that just kept giving to the boy it loved."

"I know the book." She smiled, sweetly. "I love that book."

"Me too." Malcolm inhaled deeply. "I think, in a way, Winston might have done the same thing for me. He stayed with me all this time, because I needed him to. Then, he finally knew it was okay to let go and go home…because I had found you. He knew I would be okay."

She tensed and shuffled her feet. She was purposely trying to distance herself. Why? He was certain she was feeling what he was.

She pouted. "I'm so sorry about everything that just happened with Brad…"

"I'm not."

She furrowed her brow. Damn she was cute.

"Frankly, I'm glad I saw it."

"Why?"

"Because seeing you with someone else, knowing there's the potential that someone else could hurt you…it makes me all the more certain of how I feel."

"How do you feel?"

He pulled her close and wrapped his hands around her waist. He leaned down, and kissed her gently on the lips. He pulled back and spoke in a whisper. "I feel like

I never wanna let you go, not for a second, ever again."

She threw her arms around his neck, and he kissed her completely.

****

Without breaking their kiss, Malcolm lifted her, and she straddled him, her legs tight around his waist. One of his hands held her bottom, the other, strong on her back. His one hand covered nearly her entire back, his strong muscles holding her effortlessly. Her softness made him want to protect her and overtake her—all at once. Malcolm fought to calm his breathing, he was so deep in their kiss, so connected to her, he finally understood that quote from Tolstoy...he forgot where she ended and he began. He placed her on the bed, gently, and pulled back to look at her.

"Malcolm..." Her mouth was red and puffy.

"Yeah?" Was he being totally insensitive to think she would want this? "Am I pushing too fast?" His racing heart and bulging jeans prayed she would say no.

"No, no..." She shook her head. "I—I wanted to say I'm sorry I kept a secret. That I didn't tell you I was a vet."

"Summer..." His weight jostled her on the bed as he lay next to her. He stroked her face as he spoke. "I wish you had told me, but only 'cause I think it's amazing."

Her face lit up. "Really?"

"Yes." He smiled. "And as far as worrying about it not being sexy—the fact that you're a surgeon? You're really a surgeon...?"

She nodded.

"I think it's incredibly sexy. And I get it, the reason you didn't tell me. I know what people think of me. I can only imagine what Jeanette told you." He shook his head, looking away. His eyes found their way back to hers. "So yeah, I have the reputation of dating models, but Summer, you are so much more beautiful than any other woman I have ever known."

Her eyes widened as she smiled. She blushed, turning away.

He sat up as he spoke. "And I owe you an apology."

"For what?" She shook her head.

"I was mean, back when we were on tour. I said things that were hurtful."

"It doesn't matter Malcolm, they were true."

"No." He shook his head. "It does matter. And they weren't true. I have never known anyone, model or not, who is as beautiful as you."

She scoffed.

"Don't scoff, Sum." He shook his head, hanging his hand on the back of his neck as they spoke.

She sat up, taking a deep breath.

"I wanted to go after you so many times. Countless times. Every moment of every day."

"I wanted you to." Her voice was breathy.

"I was so afraid I would never see you again…"

She nodded. "Me, too."

"I wanna be with you—always."

"I want that too, Malcolm…"

He pulled her closer, but she stopped him, putting her hands on his heart. Despite the warmth of her palms, a cold chill raced down Malcolm's spine.

"But Malcolm…we both know the reason we work, together, is because there's an end point. Brad is an asshole, but he was right. I do have to go home…to work, and to fulfill my employment contract."

"And if you don't?"

She started, pulling away, seeming surprised he could ask this. "There is no 'don't,' Malcolm. I can't afford to break or buy out the contract, and more than that, I have no other prospects. I'm relying on that job. I'm very good at what I do, but so are other people. And I've worked every day of my life—since the second grade—to get here. Even through the death of my parents, I just kept working. Like you." Her eyes dropped down, and she pushed a sigh from her mouth.

She bit her lip, and her eyes lifted to his. "I know you understand, Malcolm. The reason you've allowed yourself to be with me this summer is because you knew, deep in here…" she placed her hand on his heart, "…you knew we would have to end. You trusted there was an endpoint, a…a…finish line, and well, here we are. And the harder the ending is, the more it hurts, the better you feel. Because as long as you hate yourself for what happened to Julian, you'll never allow yourself to be happy and to really be with someone else…"

He swallowed hard, a chill overtaking his body. She was right, of course, about all of it. Damn it.

"That's why the condoms."

His eyes darted to her. "What?"

"I know you want to keep yourself safe, and your partner, too. But I also know you'll never risk having another child. I can't blame you. I can only imagine the pain you must be feeling."

He exhaled. "I don't think I'll ever be ready to have another child."

"I know." She smiled, her eyes glassing over. "I just…" She let her words fall away, and her eyes dropped down.

He placed a finger under her chin and lifted so she would look into his eyes.

"What? Sum? What were you gonna say?"

"I just hope one day you can understand moving forward isn't the same as forgetting."

She shrugged like it was nothing, but those few words she had strung together, they were more powerful than any song he had ever written, and more therapeutic than any advice he had ever received.

"I have today and tomorrow, Malcolm. Tuesday morning, I have to go back to my real life."

He nodded, a lump forming in his throat. How was it possible he had everything except the one thing he really wanted? He cleared his throat.

"I have a show Monday night. At the Garden. Stay with me through then. Be with me, completely…and…" He swallowed hard. "I'll get my driver to take you back Tuesday morning."

"Okay." She nodded.

She said exactly what he needed her to, and yet, her compliance hurt worse than any betrayal.

"Until then, Summer…"

He leaned forward and pushed her back onto the bed. She wrapped her arms around his shoulders as he kissed her over and over, his hand making its way to her top. He lifted her shirt, and placed his hand on her belly. She shuddered. He narrowed his brows, feeling something…

"Is this tape? Are you hurt?"

"No, no…" She laughed, looking at him.

He ran his fingers across her toned, beautiful belly, with just the right amount of softness. Her belly drove him wild.

"I—I haven't taken your medallion off since the second you asked me to wear it." She grimaced as she pulled on the tape.

"Let me." Malcolm pushed her hand out of the way and eased the tape off of her. He held the medal in his fist. There was a big red "X" left behind on her skin. "Ow, does it hurt?"

"Un-uh…"

He kissed the spot, and she exhaled, wiggling.

"So why'd you take it off?" He let his kisses travel all across her abdomen.

"I uh, I was going to go into surgery this morning, so I taped it to myself. That way it would still be on me, but I wouldn't lose it. I never wear jewelry, so I was worried it might unclasp during the operation."

"What kind of surgery?" His kisses moved lower on her belly as she spoke.

"A dog had a-a…uh…You know that's incredibly distracting, right?"

Malcolm looked up at her, smiling. She wiggled under his touch, and his jeans grew tighter. Her tight, soft body writhing beneath him drove him wild.

"Anyway…" She took a deep breath, "The dog had a bleeding tumor in his kidney. It's a rare surgery. I was lucky to be asked."

He stopped kissing her belly.

"But you didn't participate because of me…?"

Her hands found his hair, and she caressed him, gently. He closed his eyes.

"I wanted to be here, Malcolm. There will be other surgeries."

Malcolm nodded and resumed kissing her tummy,

but in that instant, he felt what she had tried to explain before. A life with him meant missing out on the life she had worked so hard to create...and, above all, it meant missing out on creating another life—forever.

Pushing the thought of losing her aside, Malcolm eased her out of her scrubs.

"Sorry," she whispered, her legs rubbing together as she spoke.

"For what?" His eyes devoured her plain white satin bra and panties. God, she was beautiful.

"I wasn't exactly expecting...this..." She covered her mouth when she spoke. "I would have worn something much...uh...better..."

"Summer," he slid up, hovering above her, his hands resting by her shoulders. "You just don't get it. You are stunning. You don't need any of that fancy crap. Personally, I hate it."

"Really?" She giggled. "Well then you'd love my collection of flannel pajamas. It's pretty much what I live in whenever I'm home."

"I'd love to see that." He let his weight rest against her, imagining how adorable she looked in pajamas.

"Yeah?" She squirmed beneath him.

"Yeah..."

He pushed in just the right way, and she moaned. That was it. He sat up and pulled off his t-shirt. Then he pulled her up to sitting and reached around to clasp the medal around her neck, once more.

"Malcolm...I..." She held the medal out from her body.

"Shh...keep it."

"But it's your good luck charm."

"I want you to have it. Please."

She nodded, and another wave of possessiveness left a trail of crippling pain across Malcolm's chest. He reached up to rub it away. He wanted her to wear that damned medal. He wanted her in his goddamned t-shirts. He…oh, crap. He wanted every bit of himself in every part of her. He wanted to give her everything… But what? Yes, he could buy her the world, a hundred times over. But what could he give her, really?

He reached around behind her and with one hand, unhooked her bra. He peeled the bra from her, and her breasts sprung forward—ready for him.

"Summer…" His words were guttural and earthy. He needed her right now. There would be time tonight—and tomorrow—for making love to her and making sure she was happy. But right now, right now he needed to fix everything. He needed to claim her. And her eyes told him she needed it too.

Without a word he pulled off his jeans and rolled on a cover. Her eyes widened as she watched. He slid her panties down and climbed on top of her. Carefully, but with more force than he used the last time, Malcolm pushed against her.

"Malcolm…"

Her voice was soft, and she moaned as he made his way in. She was already so wet and so hot…it was so perfect it was almost painful. He grimaced.

He hovered over her, his strong muscles flexing as she grabbed his hips and pulled him closer to her. He pressed against her, and she moaned louder.

He loved the feel of covering her—of his hard, strong, worn body on top of her soft, translucent skin. He wanted to be here always, and damn, he never wanted anyone else to be. Ever. The wave of possessiveness that washed over him drove him to the edge.

Harder he thrust into her, and still she pulled him closer. She turned her head to the side, her face tightening and releasing in time with her body. She was so perfect, he wanted this moment to last, forever... He slowed his pace and leaned down over her completely, stroking her face while he kissed her.

"Summer, baby..."

"Yes...?" Her eyes were closed, and she arched off the bed, her chest pressing against his. She leaned back, opening her eyes. She smiled, and Malcolm put his hand to his heart, certain he had never seen a more beautiful creature, ever in his life.

"Baby, I—" He wanted to. Damn. He wanted to more than anything. But how unfair would that be? Being with him only led to disaster. Why would he purposely make her unhappy? She was still so young...and sure she was smart and fucking incredible, but if he told her this today, how could he expect her to leave him the day after tomorrow? To go on with her life?

"Malcolm..." She dragged her nails down his back, pulling him closer. "I know. I do, too."

He covered her mouth with his.

Chapter Twenty-Two

Summer rolled over, smiling. She reached her hand out for Malcolm, and it landed on a piece of paper.

"What?" She sat up, her head moving, as she surveyed Malcolm's master suite. Big and empty. Where was Malcolm? She glanced at the clock on the side table—four in the afternoon. His concert began in five hours. Where was he?

She grabbed the note and winced, sore from two full days in bed with Malcolm Angel. She pulled the blanket up around her and giggled. She sat back against the pillow, reading the note.

"Hey, Babe...

I had to prep for the show. Sorry to leave without waking you, but I thought you might need your sleep. Smile. Take your time getting dressed. There's food in the fridge, but in case you can't find the refrigerator—grin—"

"Oh, ha-ha..." Summer smirked and continued reading.

"Order anything you want. There's a list by the phone in the kitchen. I have accounts everywhere. Jeanette's coming by around five to get ready with you. PLEASE don't let her choose your clothes or do your hair...you're perfect just the way you are. And if you want to wear one of my t-shirts—just a suggestion—take a look in the dresser on your side of the bed."

"My side of the bed?" It was the way he worded it, familiar and right.

"See you tonight. I've got big plans for us.

—Malcolm XO"

"Big plans?" Summer lay back, already incredibly sore. "What else could we possibly do?" She covered her face with the pillow, smiling.

Then she pulled the pillow off and stared at the ceiling, her eyes welling with tears. "What could we possibly have time to do?"

She turned to face the clock again. Four-ten. In just over twelve hours, she would have to leave Malcolm Angel, forever.

****

Summer sat in the same seat she had last time she watched Malcolm perform at Madison Square Garden. Jeanette sat next to her, adjusting her sequin halter.

"I can't believe out of everything I brought you to wear, you chose that?" Jeanette rolled her eyes. "Have I taught you nothing?"

Summer giggled. "He likes me in his shirts."

Jeanette gave Summer the once over, appraising her outfit. "It does look good on you, I've got to admit. Of course the makeup I chose helps."

"Of course." Summer smiled again.

Boom! Floodlights sliced across them as a heavy downbeat signified Malcolm's eminent arrival. An announcer's voice bellowed through the arena. When the strobe lights flashed, Summer sucked in a breath. Bubbles ran up and down her arms and fingertips, and a smile swept across her face. As band member after band member took his place on the stage, the audience hollered, and Summer held her breath. Finally, Jimmy walked out, grabbing his base guitar.

Crash! The cymbals smashed, and the band started playing as Malcolm swaggered out. The crowd roared, and people jumped to their feet. Malcolm was so sexy, his powerful arms bulged from his t-shirt, and he smiled with pure, wild, raw magnetism. Summer breathed deeply, wanting nothing more than to be with him—right there, right then, again—although she was still extraordinarily sore from the last two days of togetherness.

Malcolm held up his hand as he walked, and the band began the opening chords of one of their best known songs. The audience roared as Malcolm grabbed the mic with both hands. He looked directly at Summer and smiled. She blushed and smiled back. He grabbed the corner of his t-shirt and pointed to her.

"Nice shirt," he mouthed.

Jeanette prodded Summer with her elbow, and the two giggled as Malcolm began singing. Summer was so full and overwhelmed, she reached out and grabbed Jeanette's hand. She squeezed.

Malcolm was on fire as he played song after song. Summer beamed at him, proudly. He had never before been this edgy, this real, or this charismatic. Finally, Malcolm sang the last few notes of a fast song and cracked a water bottle, dumping it over his head. The audience howled in appreciation—especially the women. A shooting pain hit Summer in the stomach as she looked around the audience, knowing any one of these women could be in Malcolm's bed tomorrow night.

Suddenly, her mood darkened and she sat back, pouting. Malcolm cocked his head staring at her. Good grief, was he watching her reactions while he performed? Is that even feasible? Not wanting to throw him off his game, she smiled, just in case.

Slowing everything down, Malcolm sat with his guitar and strummed the first few chords of his love song. He smiled as he began to speak.

"I—uh…"

"We love you, Malcolm!"

"I love you, too…" His eyes landed on Summer as he said this, and her breath quickened as she stared back at him—lost.

The audience hollered, and Summer lifted a shaking hand to rub the pain in her stomach. Something was different tonight. But what? What was happening here?

"So—uh…"

Malcolm laughed, shaking his head, the audience laughing with him. Summer sat forward, her eyes riveted on Malcolm. He turned back to face Jimmy, and the two shared a private chuckle.

"Well…" Malcolm strummed his guitar. "So often when I sing this song, I'm asked to announce a proposal…"

The audience screamed.

"Usually, there's some poor…" he laughed, "nervous guy who decides, for some reason, he's gonna ask the woman he loves to marry him—in front of the…entire…freaking…world." Malcolm emphasized the last words, shaking his head.

The audience roared and yelled their approval.

Malcolm put up a hand and continued strumming, while Jimmy supported him quietly in the background.

Summer was so far forward in her seat, she was

nearly on her feet. Something was different about Malcolm tonight. Something…

"Let me get through this one, guys."

The audience hollered again in appreciation.

"Thank you." Malcolm nodded, looking down at his guitar. "Well tonight," he took a deep breath, smiling. "It seems I'm that…poor guy…"

The audience bellowed. A thunderous noise crashed down on Summer as she tried to understand what Malcolm was saying. Jeanette turned to Summer, but Summer couldn't tear her eyes off Malcolm. Her jaw dropped open.

He kept playing. "So…I'm not saying it makes complete sense. And I'm not saying I've got it all worked out yet—but fuck it, I will…"

He laughed again as a cacophonous noise blanketed Summer.

"What I'm saying is I'm happy for the first time in my life, and more importantly, thanks to this special woman, I know it's okay to be happy…and it's okay to be sad, and it's okay just to be me. But what's not okay is letting you go…"

The music grew louder as Summer stood and walked closer to the stage. Security stepped aside, not blocking her way.

"So, what I'd like to ask, here in front of oh, this'll go viral, so let's say, millions of people…" Malcolm chuckled, shaking his head again, "is this."

He stopped playing and set his guitar down, grabbing his mic. He stood, and the band took over playing the instrumental version of Malcolm's love song. Malcolm walked downstage and directly toward Summer. He nodded to security, and they lifted

Summer up onto the stage. Jimmy ran over and handed Malcolm a box.

"Malcolm…" Summer stood before Malcolm, her hands shaking. She stared at him, her eyes running back and forth across his.

She bit her lip, and he smiled.

"What I'd like to ask is…"

Malcolm dropped to one knee as the audience grew rowdy. People were screaming and running wild. Women fainted in the aisles as security worked to contain the chaos. Summer lifted an ice cold, shaking hand to her mouth.

"Dr. Summer Wynters…" Malcolm chuckled at her name. "I am asking in front of the entire world. Will you marry me?" He opened the ring box, and there, staring at Summer, was a perfectly plain, platinum band. "I did some research and found out you won't have to take this off while you're working…except and only, and I mean *except* and *only* when you're in surgery."

Summer nodded, feeling faint.

"So, since I wanted to buy you a really big fucking rock but thought better of it—I bought you a really big fucking ranch. Jimmy?"

Malcolm stood and pointed to the back wall of the stage. Summer turned back to see a projection of the most beautiful ranch she had ever seen.

Summer gasped, placing her hand on her heart. Her knees buckled, and she gulped a huge breath, trying to fight the dizziness. Malcolm slipped his arm around her, holding her.

"I've got you, baby." He whispered these words, only for her to hear.

She nodded, completely overwhelmed.

"Will this work for your clinic?"

She nodded again, unable to form words. She smiled at him with tears streaming down her cheeks.

"Sum?" Malcolm raised his eyebrows, questioning her, speaking into the microphone again. "Uh, I don't think you ever answered my original question. What's your answer to my proposal? Will you marry me?"

"Oh!"

She laughed, and he laughed with her as the audience went wild.

"Yes, Malcolm. A million times, yes…" She threw her arms around his neck, holding him tight.

Malcolm picked her up and spun her around. He placed her down, gently, and balancing the mic, took her face in his hands. "I love you, Summer."

"I love you, too, Malcolm."

The music swelled, and Malcolm kissed her through the entirety of the song.

Epilogue

Five Years Later

"Jeanette, you look beautiful." Malcolm embraced Jeanette as best he could, her bulging belly between them. He inhaled the fresh country air, smiling.

"Yeah?"

"Oh, yeah." Malcolm stood back. "More beautiful than I've ever seen you."

"You're a good friend, Mal…and a great liar." She rubbed her belly. "They say the second baby pops quickly but come on, this one's going to be as tall as me when it comes out."

Malcolm helped Jeanette into a chair as Sabrina, Jeanette's oldest, jumped onto his back.

"Uncle Malcolm!"

Malcolm spun her around, kissing her on the cheek. "Hey, you little monkey…"

She jumped down and faced him. "Uncle Malcolm, guess how old I am?"

"Um…Seventeen?"

"No." She stomped her foot and planted both hands on her hips.

"Fifteen?"

"No…"

Sabrina pouted, making Malcolm smile.

"I'm four."

"Are you sure?"

Jeanette's husband, Steven, walked up. He clasped Malcolm's hand, shaking it. "No making her any older than she already acts."

"What took you so long? How far away did you park?" Jeanette rolled her eyes.

"The ranch is huge, honey." Steven leaned down, kissing her and then stood back up to speak to Malcolm. "Got to love those pregnancy hormones, huh?"

A stabbing pain hit Malcolm in the stomach as he smiled, politely.

Steven backpedaled. "Oh, I mean…well, you've heard… Hey, I like the beard."

Malcolm ran his hand up over his chin. "Thanks."

"Maybe I should grow one, what do you think, honey?"

Steven was a nice guy, but he just never seemed to know when to let things drop. But Malcolm was glad Steven was with Jeanette, instead of Elijah, that scumbag business manager Malcolm used to have.

Jeanette turned to Steven. "Tell you what. You can grow a beard like Malcolm just as soon as you record your fiftieth album to go multi-platinum. Congrats by the way, Mal."

Malcolm smiled.

"In the meantime, Wall Street likes the smooth, sleek look. And so do I."

Jeanette batted her lashes, and Steven kissed her again.

Steven stood up, clearing his throat. "Thanks for having the party here again."

"My pleasure." Malcolm smiled, truly happy to be

surrounded by life.

Steven rocked on his heels. "So uh, you guys still haven't decided to take the plunge, huh?"

"Steven…" Jeanette shook her head.

And there it was. Steven was the only man Malcolm knew who never understood when to leave things alone.

Steven asked innocently, as everyone did, but still Malcolm cringed behind a smile. He twirled his wedding band around his finger. What about poor Summer? How many times did people ask her if she was ready to be a mother? Malcolm looked around their ranch. The house was massive; the grounds, impeccable. They had everything—everything money could buy. And they were completely in love. But still…were they complete?

Summer never asked, never once brought it up, but he knew she must have considered it. He watched her any number of times with Sabrina. He saw the longing in Summer's eyes when she thought he wasn't looking. She was over thirty years old now. She must be ready…although, because she loved him, she'd never say so.

Awkwardly waiting for an answer, Steven looked around the vista. It was impressive. Malcolm inhaled the rich country air. He loved it here, he was proud of the home they created. Despite everything, he never had that feeling of pride inside his multi-million dollar condo on the Upper West Side.

"Man," Steven shook his head, mercifully deciding to change the subject. "Every time I come here, I can't get over this place—the barns, the fields, even your recording studio is picturesque. Very cool. Coming from Manhattan…well, you know."

"I certainly do." Malcolm nodded.

"You guys coming back to the city anytime soon?" Steven lifted Sabrina and placed her on his shoulders as he spoke.

Malcolm smiled. "I don't know. You know, Sum…she works like mad."

"I hear she's put you to work…" Jeanette rubbed her tummy as she spoke.

"Oh yeah…" Malcolm nodded, smiling. "I love the folks around here—they have no idea who I am…" He chuckled. "This morning we visited an old woman with a sick horse who couldn't afford vet services, so she asked me if I wanted a chicken as payment." Malcolm grinned. "She said I needed to eat, because I looked like one of those 'rock and roll boys' who are too skinny." Malcolm sighed, contently.

Steven laughed. "You must like the people here, 'cause they've even got you calling them, 'folks'."

Malcolm grinned and suddenly adrenaline coursed through his veins. Summer was heading toward him. He knew it. He could feel her presence even before he saw her.

"Aunt Summer!" Sabrina shimmed off her dad's shoulders and ran up to Summer. Summer carefully laid down a box she was carrying, and in one swoop, lifted Sabrina, plopping her onto one round, full hip. A hip that was made to carry a baby.

"What's in the box?" Sabrina wiggled against Summer, and Summer laughed.

"Well, we need to ask your mom about this gift first. The rest of your gifts are for later." Summer turned to Malcolm, her face lighting up. "Could you?"

She nodded to the box.

Every time he looked at her, it was like that first time he saw her from stage.

She smirked as Malcolm grabbed the box and handed it to Jeanette.

"What is it?" Jeanette held it cautiously.

"You got me." Malcolm shrugged.

The box moved slightly, startling Jeanette. "Hey," Jeanette laughed, turning to Summer. "Don't you know better than to scare a pregnant lady?"

"Just peek inside. Carefully…" Summer bounced on her toes, excited. She bounced Sabrina along with her. Summer was so young, and beautiful, and filled with kindness and goodness. She was perfect.

Jeanette cracked the lid and peeked inside. "A frog?"

Summer walked over to Jeanette and sat on the arm of Jeanette's chair, balancing Sabrina on top of her. Sabrina peeked in the box.

"Cooolllll!"

Summer stroked Jeanette's hair. "Because you were right. For all those years…I—I never believed. But you were right. And soon it'll be time for Sabrina to kiss her own frog."

"I'm not kissing that…" Sabrina buried her face against Summer's shoulder.

Jeanette wiped a tear and embraced Summer, as much as her belly would allow. "You'd better help me keep this one alive." She mumbled through tears.

Summer laughed, tossing her hair. Malcolm stared, awestruck.

"So." Summer stood, still carrying Sabrina. "Who's ready for a party?" Summer's voice rose an octave when she spoke to the child.

"Me!" Sabrina threw both hands into the air.

Summer pointed over her shoulder. "The barn's all set up with cowgirl decorations, a cowgirl boot piñata—so we won't have a repeat of the last party when the piñata was a horse and we cried when someone hit it—and pony rides." Summer tossed Sabrina with each word she said, and the two giggled together.

Malcolm watched them with a longing he had never before experienced. Summer placed her free hand on her opposite hip, triumphantly. She was wearing a simple red knit dress with a skinny brown belt at the waist and brown boots. Her hair fell loosely around her shoulders.

Malcolm moved toward her, his eyes locked on her. "You are so beautiful…" For a moment, he forgot anyone else was there. For a second, he forgot to breathe. For eternity, he would love her.

Summer placed Sabrina on the ground, and walked straight to Malcolm. He opened his arms, and Summer laid her head on his chest. He held her tight as images of visiting Santa and teaching their kids how to ski the bunny slope raced through his mind. All too soon, she patted his chest and stood up.

"Come on, let's get this party going before Jeanette drops another one." Summer smiled sweetly at Jeanette.

Steven helped Jeanette out of the chair and they all made their way to the barn as more and more kids began showing up. Jimmy and his gang arrived, along with the rest of Malcolm's band. Summer welcomed everyone, hugging them and offering each his or her favorite beverage. She was the most thoughtful person

Malcolm had ever known.

****

Once the party was successfully underway, Malcolm spotted Summer lingering outside the barn, watching as the party hosts pinned sheriff badges to the tiny guests. She giggled.

Malcolm made his way to her, grabbing her hand. Together they watched as a small army of kids played games, their parents laughing. It was a beautiful scenario—filled with life and happiness. Summer watched, wistfully. Malcolm's heart ached when she wiped a tear.

"It's okay, Malcolm…" She turned to him and leaned back against the wall of the barn. "I don't need that. You've given me everything I've ever wanted. You've given me the world, but all I ever really wanted was you." She smiled, and there was no doubt she was an angel…his angel…Summer Angel.

"But what if I want you to have everything…?" As soon as he said the words, he realized he meant them.

"Malcolm…" She shook her head.

"What if I want everything with you?"

"What are you saying, Malcolm?" She looked up at him with her giant eyes, her lips, quivering. She was so beautiful and soft and…his…

He stood up taller, wanting her like he had never wanted her before. He pulled her farther from the entrance of the barn, and nudged her to a far wall, gently. His breath raced, and he began panting, wondering if he would have the ability to stop. He planted his forearms on either side of her, his body holding her against the wall, possessiveness taking over his being. She reached up and stroked his face with her hands.

"I'm right here, Malcolm…I promise…"

He nodded, pushing against her, holding her tighter to the wall. Suddenly the thought of her with a swollen belly…with a baby…*his* baby…growing inside, was more than he could stand. But no—he would not conceive a child, their child, against a wall of a barn.

He felt her tremble as he leaned closer to her ear. He spoke softly. "I wish I could marry you over and over again, every second of every day. I wish I could place wedding bands on every one of your fingers. I wish I could be inside you…always…claiming you…making you mine…always. I love that you're Mrs. Malcolm Angel…"

She moaned, softly, and he felt the swell in his pants. He pushed against her.

"I am yours, Malcolm…every bit of me."

"Promise me…"

"Mmm…" she moaned. "I promise, Malcolm…"

He leaned down and kissed her, his tongue taking her as the rest of him wanted to.

He pulled back and looked into those gorgeous, round eyes. "Summer, baby…I'm ready."

"I know…but the party…" Her words were barely audible. She moaned again.

"No…" He smiled and chuckled. "I mean…I'm ready."

Her eyes flew open, and she shook her head, focusing. "What?" She fought it back, but a shiny glimmer of hope flashed through her eyes.

She planted her hands on his chest. That was always the position she took when they needed to discuss something serious. He smiled.

"Malcolm, this can't be desire talking. This...you know...if we do this...there's no changing our minds. It's forever."

"We're forever."

"Yes...but..."

He knew her logical scientific mind was looking for reasons to say no, and there were plenty of them—his crazy life, her career. But none of it mattered; they would make it work, just like they always did. She knew that. But her serious expression and furrowed brow told him she was looking for a reason to say no. And she would say no, to protect him. But she didn't need to protect him anymore. Now it was his job to protect her—always and forever. He stared into her eyes and saw fear. "What is it?" He placed his forehead against hers. "Summer? Baby?"

"I'm terrified if we do this, you'll be sorry. Or blame me. Or hate me." The tears fell fast and hard.

He kissed her forehead, gently. "I wanna have a baby with you."

"Malcolm..." Her voice dropped off, and she searched his eyes, desperately.

"I wanna have a baby."

She shifted and bit her lip.

He leaned closer and whispered into her ear. "Summer...I want you to have my baby."

She looked up at him with joy in her eyes that were already heavy with lust. She threw her arms around him, hugging him fully and completely. And in that moment, he knew nothing in life mattered more than making her happy. Whatever they faced, they would face together. As they had already.

He held her tightly, lifting her off the ground,

counting the minutes until they could be together completely. Tonight, he could throw away the thin barrier of protection that protected his heart. Now, finally, there would be nothing at all between them.

He held her at arms' length, staring at her beauty. Summer Angel—his summer angel—the woman who swooped down one particularly hot summer in Manhattan to save him. And he was eternally grateful she had. There was only one thing left to say.

"Summer... Baby..."

"Yes, Malcolm?"

Her breath was hot on his neck. He held her, his strong arms tight around her tiny waist. He dropped his forehead against hers, closing his eyes.

"Thank you..."

A word from the author…

I am so excited to bring you *Summer of Irreverence*, the first book in my New York Artists series, standalone novels about strong, artistic men, and the smart, unexpected women they fall for.

I am an Amazon and Barnes and Noble bestselling author and a NYC girl at heart. I write "gritty romance," in the genres of YA, NA; women's fiction; and romance. I'm also the author of *The Letting* and *The Coupling*, books 1 and 2 of The Letting series. I began my career as an award-winning playwright, and I am a proud member of RWA, PAN. I have my BA in English and my MA in Theatre.

I believe in Luna Bars for lunch; lots of decaf coffee; running to clear my mind; yoga as often as possible; time with friends; and reading Hemingway and Bukowski. But mostly, I believe in kindness and love, especially my love for my husband and my two young girls.

To find out more about me, the New York Artists series, The Letting series, and what's coming soon, please visit: www.CathrineGoldstein.com

Thanks so much, and I hope you enjoy, *Summer of Irreverence*!

Thank you for purchasing
this publication of The Wild Rose Press, Inc.

If you enjoyed the story, we would appreciate your
letting others know by leaving a review.

For other wonderful stories,
please visit our on-line bookstore at
www.thewildrosepress.com.

For questions or more information
contact us at
info@thewildrosepress.com.

The Wild Rose Press, Inc.
www.thewildrosepress.com

Stay current with The Wild Rose Press, Inc.

Like us on Facebook

https://www.facebook.com/TheWildRosePress

And Follow us on Twitter
https://twitter.com/WildRosePress